PRAISE FOR THE UNSOLVABLE CIRCUS

"It has been a while since I last read a book that made me laugh as much as this one."
Marios Yiannakou

*****

"This is a very entertaining book that pulled a few good laughs out of me..." A. A. Alvarez, Author

*****

"...I look forward to future works from this talented author." Addie Bishop, Author

DAVID J. HORN'S

HARD LABOR

HORN PUBLISHING

First Edition
Published in the United States by Horn Publishing.

ISBN: 978-0-9847502-0-7

For all the working stiffs
who can't stand working.

Hard Labor

Table of Contents

Before We Begin...

J amie Dropping, unearthed inexplicably, finds his *terra firma* existence inhospitable. If asked, he would describe his life as if he were living in exile. On the road. A stranger. A stray dog unable to find his way home. Lost. As a consequence, he always feels somehow foreign and always out of place.

His life is filled with road blocks, pitfalls, booby traps and diversions. He feels mired in his own sludgy existence. Yes, he rebels against the muck, he labors hard for freedom from the mud that he believes infects his waking moments, but he never manages to actually reach

Higher Ground nor does he ever experience the Divine Rain that will wash him clean. He always remains the victim of the silent and invisible law that governs his universe: sludge increases with time, filling all available space. By the end, his life is so constipated with muck and glop that the only way to be purged of the filth is through death. Death, according to this law, is the Great Laxative.

*****

Yes, Jamie Dropping is an incredible cynic.

*****

He popped out of the literary womb at the ripe age of 37 with a sagging waistline, a coffee stain on his shirt, receding hair line and wrinkled khakis. He was born with an already tarnished heart and a moth eaten soul. He was tired, frustrated and he made sure not to think too much about reality.

Since his rather uneventful birth, Jamie Dropping has been bouncing around in literary-time, aging and un-aging. One minute he is twenty two years old, working for Gipta Temporary Agency, the next he is thirty three years old, working for OOPS, Inc. And in the end, he is a life insurance salesman at the end of time. Oh, how dolefully ironic.

*****

It is true that at some point in his youth he listened to the faint whisper of the Great Unknown. As a boy he knew that he was born to search for something that he could not define. But as he grew older he realized that the search would have to be sacrificed for the sake of Duty. The Big Questions of his adolescence were a waste of time. *What does it all mean?* Jamie would rather think about the final scores of football games. He surrendered himself to the struggle of the office. And at some unobservable point in time, as quietly as the summer slips into the fall, Jamie Dropping began to live his life without really living his life at all. He played the part of a machine, operating on muscle memory. And by the end, he is merely doing his job, dutifully performing his Hard Labor.

*****

THE JOB INTERVIEW

The interview is beginning to attract flies, thought Jamie Dropping. Sitting across from Jamie was Mick Schmuk who didn't really want a job, but he did need money, "Don't you want to take notes?" Mick Schmuk also sincerely believed that his words deserved to be preserved in written form. Jamie Dropping didn't necessarily agree. He thought that Mick Schmuk had the intellect of a glass of lukewarm water. But he decided to humor him. He picked up a red pen and pretended to write while Mick Schmuk dragged his moldy past from the closet. Jamie listened and doodled – circles, parallelograms and triangles.

"...and then when I was eleven, my dad drove us to

Florida to visit his family. It was an awful trip. I remember my uncle. He was nuts. He thought he was a rabbit. He wore this gray velveteen bunny costume all the time. He lived with my grandmother and she was pretty sad that her son thought he was a rabbit. They lived off of her social security which wasn't much. He could only find work around Easter time..."

*****

Jamie had once skimmed an article in a **National Geographic** about the caste system in India. It featured a story about an untouchable who worked as a human roto-rooter. Wearing little more than a loincloth, this poor guy slid through a sewer system in Bombay making sure that the shit could flow freely.

The article didn't make Jamie feel angry about human injustice; nor did he feel pity for the untouchable or other untouchables like him. But it did make Jamie reevaluate his own occupational angst. He, like 91.4% of all working people, detested his job. Work made his life seem pointless and pathetic.

But after reading the article, Jamie felt fortified in the knowledge that no matter what existential demons plagued him between the hours of 9 and 5, at least he wasn't forced to play Tarzan of the Sewer System.

*****

"Do you know about Adam and Eve?" Mick Schmuk had hijacked the interview and they were fast approaching the Garden of Eden.

Jamie decided he would try to put the interview back on track, "What kind of job are you looking for?"

Mick Schmuk pondered the question for a brief moment, crossing his thin legs. His socks were slouched around his ankles, and Jamie could see the milky white calf of his right leg. "I want a nice desk job with lots of coffee breaks."

Cyberslacking. That's what Mick Schmuk wanted to do. It wasn't the type of answer that inspired confidence, but this man sitting across from Jamie was strangely serious. Mick Schmuk, like his signature on his application, was a scribble of a man. Frazzled chestnut hair and tired eyes. He resembled an overused eraser: run down and worn out. He was a lonely guy, and you could smell the silence on him. Jamie was sure that Mick Schmuk lived a lonely muted existence in some drab apartment.

Then Mick Schmuk continued, "My father always told me that Adam was a deadbeat. He lay around in Eden eating fruit and having sex with Eve. He was a real freeloader. One day, God had enough so he told Adam to go get a job. He kicked him out of Eden and sentenced him to a life of hard labor..." Jamie rolled his eyes and continued doodling.

"...but God gave Eve the real kick in the crotch. She would hurt like hell whenever she gave birth. Wham! Right in the kisser. Even giving birth would become a labor."

There was a pause. Mick Schmuk was pondering thoughts he had never thought before. "Maybe God had been kicked out of some godly paradise by a bunch of other gods because he broke some stupid rule. Maybe God was sentenced to a life of labor just like he sentenced

Adam to a life of labor? Maybe the universe is one big crappy punishment..."

Jamie looked down at his doodle. A stick figure had hung himself from an apple tree.

*****

Jamie had been working for the Gipta Temporary Agency for three long and dreadful years. The office was located on South Normal Street, sandwiched between a funeral home and a bar. Work, drink and death. Jamie found it profoundly poetic: we work to keep our minds off of death, drink because we hate our jobs, but always bite it in the end.

The Gipta Temporary Agency, compared to the funeral home, was a dreary and hopeless place. Some witty delinquents had underlined the misery of the office by spray painting the words "Butt Acres" across the front wall. The words had been painted over, but they still lived underneath the fresh coat of paint, and if you looked hard enough you could still see the spirit of the words lingering behind.

Inside Gipta Temporary Agency things weren't much better. The windows were streaked with white grime, the walls were lemon yellow, the rug was blood red and the place always reeked of burnt coffee (which Jamie was certain was also the same odor as souls burning in hell).

*****

Jamie was the only employee at the Gipta Temporary Agency. The only other person that "worked" there was Sam Gipta, the owner. Sam was in his early forties and he bore the telltale signs of living a happily married existence: he was always on edge, cynical, extremely tired and his midsection was actively rebelling against the waistline of his pants. In fact Sam's pants were moving south along with his waistline, and his shirttails were moving north. He paced around the office, burdened with dreams of success and visions of failure – a frenzy of shirt tucking and pant hiking activity.

*****

Once, Jamie caught Sam and his business parter, George, strangling a turkey. Jamie was in the middle of an interview when a sound like Satan gargling made it impossible to continue. He went to Sam's office. The door was closed as usual, but he could hear Sam amidst a squall of gobbling, "I can't do it."

George instructed, "Sam, remember what Dr. Vilegas told us."

Jamie pushed the door open. Sam was seated at his desk with a turkey on his lap. Both hands were wrapped around the turkey's neck. The turkey flapped its wings desperate for life – feathers flying everywhere. The bird knew damn well that the end was near.

On Sam's desk sat a bottle of uncapped rum and two cheap cigars smoldered in an ashtray. Between the rum and the ashtray was an enormous silver cleaver.

"Is everything OK, Sam?" Jamie asked.

Sam said nothing. He and George exchanged blank looks. Then Sam said, "The bank's got me by the balls."

Jamie didn't understand the relationship between the bank and the turkey, so he stated the obvious, "Sam, there's a turkey on your lap."

Again, George and Sam stared at each other. Eventually George explained, "We couldn't find a rooster."

At that very moment it became clear to Jamie that things were not *alright* at the Gipta Temporary Agency. Things were far from *alright*. "Listen, do you guys think you could keep the turkey quiet until I finish this interview?"

"He shouldn't be making noise for much longer," winked George.

Jamie closed the door and went back to his desk. He wasn't sure what was going on, but it looked as though Sam had been reduced to the murder of poultry, in some sort of black magic-ish, voodoo-economic ceremony, and all for the bottom line.

*****

Jamie had a stack business cards – he never handed them out to anyone – and each silently insisted in the top drawer of his desk that he was an *Occupational Fulfillment Director*. Jamie instinctively understood that an exotic title was like wearing a cheap disguise. He had even read somewhere, although he couldn't remember where (perhaps it was a fortune from a fortune cookie), "Ridiculous jobs hide behind fancy titles." Maybe he hadn't read it anywhere. Anyway, it was the truth. He believed his job was more pathetic than wiping the asses of the dead. He found jobs for people who really weren't interested in working. Or perhaps more accurately, they weren't interested in working for long.

Most of the people that came looking for a job were like Mick Schmuk. They spent their days watching reruns of *Happy Days* and eating Frosted Flakes. They dreamt of easy money – winning the lottery, a quick lawsuit, an appearance on a game show. But Hell is Money, and the jobs that the Gipta Temporary Agency had to offer usually involved manual labor – sweat and toil. Factory positions – inserting glass eyes into the heads of baby dolls – and a lot of warehouse jobs – loading and unloading boxes from trucks. But it was getting harder and harder to find people who wanted to lift boxes. And Mick Schmuk surely didn't want to lift any boxes.

*****

"Mr. Schmuk, I don't think that we have anything that will fit your profile at this time, but I'll keep your application on file, and as soon as something comes up, I'll give you a call," Jamie explained.

"What do you mean?" Jamie sensed anger.

He thought that his meaning was more than sufficiently clear. Mick Schmuk's nostrils flared. Then the phone rang.

Jamie answered the phone, "Gipta Temp Agency."

A voice rasped, "What the hell is wrong with you?" It was Mrs. Rogers. She ran an office supply company and was always on the brink of a heart attack. "This woman you sent me should be in the loony bin, not in my office. She doesn't do any work. All she does is walk around saying the Hail Mary."

"She's probably very religious."

"Religious?   She's freaking out the God damned customers."

It was only 10 am and Jamie already felt a headache

~17~

revving its engines. "I can send a replacement tomorrow," he said.

"What the hell will she do? Sit in the corner and meditate?"

"No. *He'll* sell pencils to the pencil-less."

Mrs. Rogers slammed down the phone.

Jamie hung up. Mick Schmuk was still irritated. "I spent all this time talking with you, and now *you* decide that you don't have a job for *me*?" He seemed insulted.

"Mr. Schmuk, as luck may have it, a position just opened up. You can start tomorrow."

Jamie smiled a withered smile.

Mick Schmuk folded his arms and sank into a frown. He sighed a sigh of mortal despair. "I want to get something straight. First there is no job and now there is a job?"

"The telephone call was from a client. She wants someone new," explained Jamie.

"And you expect me to believe that?"

"It's the truth."

Mick Schmuk scoffed, "Do you want to know something? You're just some kid that doesn't know what the hell he's doing." He was simmering with rage. "I want to speak to your manager."

Jamie was stunned silent. Never had anything like this happened to him before. He studied Mick Schmuk for a moment. He looked like the type of person who could easily *go postal*: a lonely, homely, extremely shortsighted loser who fantasized about killing the people that made him miserable.

Jamie didn't have the stamina nor the courage necessary to argue with Mick Schmuk, so he trudged off to Sam's office.

*****

Sam was pacing as usual, but he looked particularly dire: unwashed, desperate and sweaty.

"Sam there's this guy who wants to complain about me."

Sam pulled at his collar and wrestled his shirt into his sagging pants. "How old is he?"

"In his thirties."

"Does he have a family?"

"He has an uncle who thinks he's a rabbit."

Sam peered at Mick Schmuk from behind his office door. "No one would miss this bastard."

"He's a real pain in the ass," agreed Jamie.

"Here's what we'll do. You distract him and I'll hit him on the head with this..." Sam looked around his office for something heavy – something to clobber someone with, "...with this phonebook."

Jamie was pleasantly surprised by Sam's managerial instinct to protect him. He felt a warmness for him that he had never felt before. It was almost a father-son moment. They both watched Mick Schmuk from behind the door to Sam's office, two pairs of spying eyes.

*****

The idea of hitting Mick Schmuk with a phonebook sounded completely rational but in an irrational way. But Jamie had doubts, "I don't really think you need to hit him though..." but Sam wasn't listening.

"Jamie, after I killed the turkey things have gotten really bad. My wife left me, my car was stolen twice, and now I've been diagnosed with cancer." Sam continued watching Mick Schmuk from behind the door. "Dr. Vilegas said I need to find *larger prey* in order to reverse the effects of the turkey. This is about life and death, Jamie."

"So, you want to kill this guy?"

"It's not really killing. It's sacrificing. The Incas and the Aztecs used to do it all time. Me and George were actually planning on sacrificing you. That's why you haven't been fired yet."

"Oh," Jamie didn't know what else to say.

*****

Sam's sudden confession that Jamie was a candidate for human sacrifice was troubling, to say the least. Jamie felt as though the rug of reality had been pulled out from under his feet. Everything seemed suddenly blurry, strangely out of focus, shrouded in mysterious smoke and bizarre carnival shadows. He felt betrayed by reality. *The real* was just a sham, a cardboard facade, a cheap disguise. For the last three years he had thought that he had been doing his job in a lackluster, unspectacular yet diligent manner, and everything was more or less alright. But now he knew the *truth*. His boss hadn't fired him because he wanted to *sacrifice* him. *Thank God for Mick Schmuk*, thought Jamie.

Jamie trudged to his desk, Sam Gipta followed. When they arrived at Jamie's desk, they found Mick Schmuk on the edge of his seat, tingling with gut wrenching passive aggressive tension.

~20~

"Mr. Schmuk this is my boss, Sam Gipta," blurted Jamie.

"I want to complain about him," he sprang to his feet and pointed a crooked finger at Jamie.

"Hey, what's that?" asked Sam, pointing in the direction of one of the windows, opaque with white grime.

Mick Schmuk turned and looked as well. "I don't see..."

The phonebook came down with a thud. Mick Schmuk fell to his knees. He looked at Sam over his shoulder – his eyes filled with horror. "What the hell is going on here?"

Sam raised the phone book above his head for the second blow. Mick Schmuk cringed and moaned, "OK, I'll take the lousy job..."

Down came the second blow.

*****

Mick Schmuk was finally unconscious, which took quite a few blows from the phonebook. George arrived out of breath; he had sprinted the twenty feet from the parking lot to the office building.

"I got here as fast as I could," he panted. "Let's take him to the storage room," Sam suggested.

George and Sam acted quickly. They kicked off their shoes. They tied Mick Schmuk's hands and feet with their socks and shoelaces. Then the three men pulled Mick Schmuk by his ankles into the storage room.

The storage room was cinder block gray, windowless and lit up with flickering fluorescent lights. There were some metal shelves with a spartan selection of office supplies: some notebooks, a couple boxes of ballpoint pens (black and blue), post-it notes of various sizes shapes and colors, and a single box of staples.

The men dragged Mick Schmuk to a corner and left him there in a heap. George and Sam started arguing about who should *sacrifice* Mick Schmuk. Neither was born to play the role of killer. George claimed that Sam had no choice. Sam countered that the whole turkey sacrifice was all George's idea, so George should *sacrifice* Mick Schmuk. Then Sam suggested that maybe Mick Schmuk could be woken up and given a glass of poisoned water which started a debate about agency in the act of killing. While the two argued, Jamie inched his way slowly towards the door, trying hard to remain inconspicuous. He wanted no part of this drama.

Mick Schmuk began to stir, "Where am I?" He mumbled.

"Don't worry Mr... what's his name?" George asked Jamie.

"Mick Schmuk," Jamie said.

"Don't worry Mr. Schmuk. Nothing is going to happen to you."

"Then why am I tied up? And why the hell did he beat me with the phonebook?"

"Um...um..." Sam stuttered.

"He stopped taking his meds and he lost control of himself," explained George.

"But I'm back on them again," added Sam.

"Yeah. Everything will be fine. We'll untie you in just a second."

George leaned over to Sam and whispered, "What are you waiting for? You know what Dr. Vilegas said. You have to kill this bastard."

*****

Mick Schmuk was paralyzed with fear. His heart was pounding so loudly that he could barely make out the whispered words that passed between George and Sam, but he was certain that one of the words uttered was *kill*. He was sure of it. The word *kill* had fallen from George's lips like an airplane plummeting in flames to the earth. His heart started beating faster, his body shuddered.

"Did he just say *kill?* I wanna go home. I've had enough of this crap."

"Good God, no one wants to kill anyone. We want to *hire* you," explained Sam.

"That's right. *Sam* wants to *hire* you," George said soothingly.

"Well, actually, I was thinking that *you'd hire* him," Sam told George.

"Me? But I don't have any openings."

"Well, me neither," added Sam.

"JESUS CHRIST SAM. THIS WHOLE MESS STARTED BECAUSE YOU HAD TROUBLE KI..." George swallowed the word *kill*, "because you couldn't HIRE the frigging turkey."

There was a dark and defeated silence.

"You two bastards are scaring the hell out of me...and...and it's all that idiots fault," Mick Schmuk spat his words in the direction of Jamie who had managed, inch by inch to arrive at the doorway. He was only two steps

~23~

from freedom. "He's pissed off because I know he sucks at his job."

All eyes turned to Jamie.

"Jamie, where are you going?" asked George.

"I was...going...to get...a knife."

"KNIFE? HELP! SOMEONE SAVE ME!"

"Oh, for God's sake," huffed George.

"Jamie," shouted Sam. "Give me one of your socks."

"HEEELLLLLLPPPPP HELLLLLLLPPPPPP," wailed Mick Schmuk.

Jamie did as he was told. He untied his shoe and pulled off a sweaty sock. Sam wrestled with Mick Schmuk's screaming and writhing head. He spit and bit Sam's fingers, but Sam persisted and he finally managed to shove the sock into Mick Schmuk's mouth; Mick Schmuk gagged, choked and began groaning.

There was another dark and defeated silence.

Sam, George and Jamie had no idea what to do next. They were three actors with a bum script. They stood silently watching Mick Schmuk squirm and kick on the floor.

Then a voice shattered the silence. It came from the front office, "Hello. Is anyone here?"

"Oh shit," sighed George.

"Jamie go and get rid of whoever that is," whispered Sam.

*****

Jamie slipped out of the storage room and closed the door behind him softly. He turned and saw a man dressed in jeans wearing a faded T-shirt that read *No school, No work, No problem!* pacing back and forth in the front of the office.

He was thin and wiry, built like a scarecrow. He had a golden canine tooth and his gaze lurked behind black sunglasses. He had been baptized Vincent DeSchulio, but everyone that mattered in Vincent's life called him *The Shoe* – Vincent, or Vin, *The Shoe* DeSchulio.

Jamie watched The Shoe and wondered what the hell he should do. He needed to get rid of this guy. Or maybe he should have this guy go get the cops? Maybe, just maybe, The Shoe could save him from this predicament. Then The Shoe spotted Jamie, "I'm here for a fuckin' job."

Jamie approached The Shoe and said loudly, "I'M SORRY, SIR, BUT ALL THE POSITIONS HAVE BEEN FILLED." Then Jamie stopped at his desk and he began to scribble a note, *My boss has gone crazy and is going to kill...*

Vincent The Shoe exploded, "Since I've been outa jail I've gone to fifty interviews and it's all the same shit. We don't got a job for you. Well, listen you little turd, I'm not asking you for a job, I'm telling your stupid ass that your gonna find me a job."

Jamie stopped writing and looked at The Shoe. He pointed a .22 at Jamie.

Jamie tried to smile, but he was exhausted. He had unwittingly escaped being the victim of a murder and now he had stumbled right back into the role of potential murderee. *What a crappy day*, thought Jamie Dropping.

*****

The Shoe was a miserable man. His soul was a

plague of cockroaches and bitter sores. Most of his troubles were caused by his lack of money and his phenomenally bad decisions, which usually went hand in hand. Like the time he had stolen his brother's prosthetic leg and sold it for $50. His brother tried to kill him after that, which didn't really bother The Shoe because he hated his brother, but The Shoe was pissed because he knew he could have gotten at least $150 for that leg.

The Shoe arrived at the Gipta Temporary Agency out of desperation. He knew that a job wasn't going to make him rich, nor did he believe that a job would help him deal with the loneliness and desperation of his life, but it could possibly introduce him to a whole new group of chumps, losers, gullible saps and hopefully a few babes. Potential victims.

Jamie tried to hand the note to The Shoe, but he didn't want any part of it. "I don't want that damn piece a paper. I want a job. You can't find a job for me, then I'll shoot you."

"There's an opening at this office supply store."

"Do I get to work the cash register?"

"I don't think so, but I can ask. Um...I just need to call the owner of the store." Jamie dialed the number. Busy signal. "It's busy."

"I got all day," smiled The Shoe, who possessed as much patience as hand grenade. But he felt satisfied with how things were working out. He had found a job. What was another couple minutes? He was about to stuff his gun back into his pants when he noticed that Jamie was only wearing one shoe.

The Shoe sensed the irony of the situation: his nickname and Jamie's lack of footwear. And nothing made The Shoe more irate than ironic jabs at his nickname. The Shoe suffered from acute paranoia and he knew that the irony was premeditated. It made him feel like shooting Jamie, but instead he growled, "How come you only got one shoe on?"

"I took it off so that my sock could be used to gag a man that my boss wants to kill," Jamie whispered, trying desperately to hand the note to The Shoe.

"You think I'm some kinda asshole or somethin'?"

"Of course not." Then Jamie pointed in the direction of the storage room and mouthed the syllables, "MUR DER."

The Shoe was certain that Jamie was subnormal. "Call that office supply place again," he said pointing the gun at Jamie.

Jamie sighed, picked up the phone and dialed the number. "Still busy."

Then The Shoe saw the phonebook on the floor. "How come the phonebook is laying on the floor like that?"

"My boss used it to beat a man unconscious," whispered Jamie.

The Shoe's ten seconds of patience had expired. "Do you want me to shoot you? I'll shoot you right now if that's what you want, you little smart ass."

The Shoe sidled up to the phonebook. It was in the middle of the floor, flung open to a random page. But The Shoe didn't believe in randomness. He didn't believe in much of anything. But he did believe that everything happened for a reason, although usually a pretty shitty one. He nudged the phonebook with the toe of his sneaker. It was open to a full page ad for a psychiatrist named Dr. Jerry Rammer. The ad asked, "Is your job killing you? Is work murder? Dr. Jerry Rammer can help with just one phone call." Dr. Jerry Rammer had a greasy, thumbs-up smile, his eyes had the gleam of dollar signs.

The Shoe ripped the page out of the book. "I may just need that."

Jamie stood at his desk saying nothing. The Shoe scratched his head with his gun and asked, "You ain't one of those foot perverts are you?" The Shoe had seen all sort of sick and twisted porno in his life. He had even seen a porno full of chubby CEOs, limp corporate types and sniveling lawyers sipping whiskey and smoking cigars while women rubbed their naked feet all over them. *Disgusting,* just recalling those images filled The Shoe with the desire to maim.

"No. I'm not a foot pervert," mumbled Jamie.

Then a stifled moan floated from the storage room.

"What the hell was that?" said The Shoe.

Then The Shoe saw the two other pair of shoes. He smiled darkly, "You are a foot pervert and you got a couple buddies in there waiting to play footsie, huh? That's why you're busting my balls. You just wanna get rid of me so you can go have someone rub their smelly feet all over you. You're a fuckin' sick bastard."

Jamie said, nothing. There was nothing else to say. He just sighed.

*****

The Shoe possessed a crippled sense of humor and he did not tolerate being made a fool of, and he felt especially silly asking foot perverts for a job. When The Shoe felt like a fool, he felt vulnerable and feeling vulnerable made him violent. He kicked open the door to the storage room. George and Sam froze, petrified with fear. "What the hell is going on in here?" demanded The Shoe.

"Who the hell are you?" George asked.

"None of your fuckin' business."

"Jamie, what is going on here? Who is this guy?"

"He's the new salesman at Mrs. Roger's office supply store," Jamie explained.

"Great, but why is he here? And why does he have a gun for Christ's sake?"

"I got a gun because you never know when you're gonna run into a bunch of foot perverts playing footsie in a closet."

"I have no idea what he's talking about," admitted George.

Sam didn't utter a word. He stood as silent as a wax mannequin, his heart pounding, staring at his hands.

"You guys are a bunch of foot perverts," spat The Shoe.

"Yeah, that's right we're foot perverts. So if you don't mind, why don't you get back to the office supply store," said George trying to dismiss The Shoe as quickly as possible.

"And that guy," The Shoe pointed his gun in the direction of Mick Schmuk, "he likes to be tied up?"

"Exactly, now if you don't mind..."

"He looks a little dead," The Shoe added.

Sam, looked at the floor and said, "I killed him. I strangled him to death."

"What?" said Jamie.

"Foot pervert murderers? What the hell's wrong with you guys?" asked The Shoe.

"My doctor said that I had to kill somebody," explained Sam lifelessly.

"Your doctor?" The Shoe had never heard of doctors prescribing murder. It didn't sound like a bad idea actually.

"Are you two fuckin' with me?"

"It's the truth. Jamie, tell this man about Dr. Vilegas."

"It's true. They were going to sacrifice me."

"Man this is fucked up. You guys are fuckin' crazier than the guys in the joint."

"You've been to prison?" asked George. His eyes lit up with hope.

"Yeah."

George and Sam looked at each other, they silently synchronized their thoughts, and then turned their attention to Vin The Shoe DeSchulio. "Maybe you could help us get rid of the body."

"Listen, I got a parole officer. I can't...all I want is a fuckin' job that doesn't involve committing a crime."

"We'll pay you," insisted Sam. "You see, we didn't really plan this too well. I mean the killing part wasn't so difficult, but what the hell do we do with the body?"

"Man I am not getting involved in this bullshit. All I wanted was a lousy job...collecting shopping carts...washing dishes...shit like that."

"It's just like a job. You do this work for us and we pay you."

The Shoe took a deep breath and exhaled, "I want ten grand."

"Will you take a check?" asked Sam who had $275.68 in his checking account.

*****

"Who do I make the check out to?" asked Sam.

"Make it payable to Vincent The Shoe DeSchulio."

Sam signed the check and handed it to The Shoe. The Shoe held the baby blue check in his hands, admiring the number. $10,000. He had never seen so many zeroes in a number before in his life. He folded the check neatly and put it in his back pocket.

"The best plans are always the simplest," he said as he looked out the back door of the office. Behind the Gipta Temporary Agency was a parking lot that was used by the funeral home next door. A hearse sat ominously parked next to a beige Plymouth Sundance. The Shoe had an idea. He smiled to himself, satisfied with the plan.

"OK, here's what we'll do. We're gonna carry this guy over there to the funeral home, and stick him in a coffin."

George and Sam had their doubts. Carrying a dead body into a funeral home didn't seem like such a good idea. Plus they were both hoping that the Shoe would take care of the body all by himself.

"I don't know," said Sam.

"Me either," said George.

"I was hoping that you would get rid of the body," added Sam.

"Yeah," agreed George. "If we have to help carry the body I think that ten grand is a bit steep. How about $7,500?"

The Shoe, irritated with Sam and George's haggling, growled, "You two cheapskates ain't got a choice. We sneak the stiff into the place, find a fuckin' coffin and stick him in it. It could be weeks before they find the body. It's a great fuckin' plan. You wanna know why it's a great fuckin' plan? Because it's simple."

"But someone will find the body," said Sam.

"When you get rid of a body, you don't usually want other people to find it," George added.

"When they find this stiff, they'll just think he's some asshole that needs to be buried."

Sam shook his head, "I don't know..."

"I'm not completely sold on this plan," admitted George.

"Well fuck you. There ain't no other plan. So, I'm gonna go check if the coast is clear. When I give the signal then you guys bring the body."

All negotiations ended. The Shoe, strolled out into the parking lot.

*****

"This guy is a Godsend. I really believe that everything is going to be OK now, Sam. You'll see. You'll get better, Cindy will come back to you, business will start picking up," George patted Sam on the shoulder.

"Yeah, he's a sign. And you know something else, I already feel better. Honestly, I feel healthier. Dr. Vilegas was right after all."

The three men watched The Shoe in silence as he glided about the parking lot checking the back of the hearse.

"He's got an awful nickname though," said George.

"I agree," Sam added.

"But, you know, he seems to be the type of guy that probably thinks life without a nickname really sucks. He's probably happy just to have a nickname," said Jamie.

George and Sam nodded in silence.

*****

The three men watched The Shoe strolling around the parking lot. He turned and faced them. They readied themselves, lifting Mick Schmuk's lifeless body off the ground, waiting anxiously for the signal. The Shoe smiled, his gold tooth gleaming in the sun. He gave them the finger and took off.

"That son of a bitch," said Sam.

"What a shitty fucking thing to do," whined George.

As The Shoe disappeared, Jamie couldn't help but think that this was the worst day in his short professional life. He had found out that he was a potential murderee, then forced to take part in a murder, held at gun point and nearly murdered a second time, and now he was stuck having to help his boss get rid of a dead body. And all this because his boss was practicing voodoo economics.

Things couldn't possibly get worse.

*****

The atmosphere inside the storage room was bleak. The Shoe's running away had sucked the hope of getting away with murder from the room, a metaphorical kick in crotch.

"OK guys, it's up to us now. We've got no choice. We'll have to do this by ourselves," coached George. He stood up, took a deep breath then stepped out the back door of the office. He ran over to the funeral parlor. Sam and Jamie watched as he peeked through a window. When they saw George hustling back, they quickly grabbed Mick Schmuk: Jamie took him under the armpits, Sam grabbed a leg.

"I didn't see anyone," panted George.

The three men lifted Mick Schmuk and rushed him next door.

*****

They entered the funeral home through the back door and found themselves in a long narrow hallway.

"Find a coffin," whispered Sam.

Jamie opened the door closest to him. Inside the room was an open casket. A man in a mule grey suit, made up to seem less dead and more alive lay inside the casket. The room was quiet in a creepy way, filled with the silence of vacant folding chairs. "In here," said Jamie. They rushed the body into the room.

Taped to the wall behind the casket hung a large sign, "We'll Miss You Howard," and next to the casket was a large photo collage with pictures of the dead man in his youth, children on his lap. The dead man at parties, baptisms, weddings, at the beach, drinking a beer, gradually getting older and smiling less frequently, grey haired and sitting in a wheel chair. In the center of the collage was the name *Howard Hope*.

George stayed at the door keeping a lookout for other people. He whispered the instructions, "Put him in there with that other guy." Sam and Jamie did as they were told and they lifted Mick Schmuk and dropped him into the casket.

"George, this guy's name is Hope. It's a sign. There's hope, George," explained Sam with a dreamy grin.

"Just close the lid of the coffin," said George.

Sam and Jamie tried to close the lid of the casket, but it wouldn't close. They struggled and struggled, trying to force the door shut. Sam even lay on top of the casket door trying to use his weight to close it, but it was no good.

"Take him out," said George.

They pulled Mick Schmuk out.

"Take the other guy out too."

Sam and Jamie pulled the body of Howard Hope from the casket as well.

"Now what?" hissed Jamie.

"Put the guy Sam killed in the coffin."

They picked up Mick Schmuk and swung him into the casket. Mick Schmuk rolled onto his side.

"What the hell are we going to do with the other body?"

"Put him on top of the other guy, so no one will see him," whispered George.

"But we can't close the coffin if they're both in it," protested Sam.

George looked about the room. There was a small coat closet against the wall of the room. "Try sticking him in that closet."

"We should put Mick Schmuk in the closet, and this guy back in the coffin." Jamie tried to pull Mick Schmuk out by the legs. He managed to pull him halfway out, his legs stuck out from the casket, and he was completely face down.

"We're wasting too much time. Stick the other guy in the closet," demanded George.

Jamie stopped pulling at Mick Schmuk and he helped Sam with Howard Hope.

Sam whispered to Jamie, "Dr. Vilegas was right, there's hope. Everything will be fine." Jamie felt like punching Sam in the balls as he helped him push Howard Hope into the closet. Hope refused to stay in the closet, though. He kept falling forward, pushing the doors open.

"Oh this is a great plan," said Jamie. But he and Sam kept at it. They pushed and pushed.

"God is he heavy," said Sam. "Dead weight..." and then suddenly Sam collapsed.

"Oh, shit," George ran to Sam and fell to his knees. "Sam is having a heart attack. We got to get the hell out of here."

Sam wheezed what were to be his last words into George's ear, "It was all your fault, you and that...tur...key."

George grabbed Sam under the armpits and began to

drag him out of the room. Jamie tied Howard Hope up using a couple of beige windbreakers. He closed the doors and they stayed shut. He sighed a sigh of relief and then ran out of the room. George was nowhere to be seen. Jamie rushed to the back door and as he pushed it open, two steps from freedom, a soft voice asked, "Can I help you?"

Jamie turned around. The funeral director was a short lady with a grandmotherly face. She had short grey hair, large brown rimmed glasses and a sympathetic smile.

Jamie wiped the sweat from his forehead. "I'm here for the funeral."

*****

The funeral director, Ms. Sweeney, escorted Jamie into a room adjacent to where both Howard Hope and Mick Schmuk were stashed. Separating the two rooms was a large white accordion door.

"Would you like a glass of water?"

"No," blurted Jamie. "I'm in a bit of a hurry."

"Well the family should be here any moment now. Were you close to Mr. Hope?"

"I just met him."

She looked at Jamie sympathetically. "It is never easy when someone passes."

"That's the truth."

"You'll have to excuse me while I attend to some last minute arrangements," said Ms. Sweeney who wanted to place some lilies around the casket.

Jamie sank into a chair and nearly began to weep. Ms. Sweeney made her way towards the viewing room,

~37~

ready to push open the accordion doors when a small, noisy mob entered the funeral parlor.

Jamie jumped to his feet and hoped to remain unnoticed as the small crowd of mourners, children, grandchildren, nieces, nephews of Howard Hope staggered into the room. The group was like a black blot of ink spilled onto a piece of paper, black suited, blue ties, black veils, black shoes. In the center of the crowd, being supported by a couple of young boys was an old wispy haired lady: Howard Hope's sister, Gertrude.

"OH MY GOD. MY BABY BROTHER. MY BABY BROTHER," wailed Gertrude. "IT AIN'T FAIR. I SHOULD HAVE BEEN FIRST, HOWARD. NOT YOU..."

"This is my Aunt Gertie, she just flew in from Pittsburgh," someone from the group explained to Ms. Sweeney.

Ms. Sweeney held out her hand and said softly, "I'm sorry for your loss." Aunt Gertie took the soft hand of Ms. Sweeney and looked about the room. Her eyes landed on Jamie. "Who the hell is that jagoff?"

There was an uncomfortable silence. Jamie made no effort to explain his presence, so Ms. Sweeney attempted an introduction, "He's one of your brother's friends, I believe." Jamie tried to avoid making eye contact with any of the mourners and then Aunt Gertie roared, "AHHHHHH HOWARD."

Ms. Sweeney then asked the mourners, "Would you like to see Howard?"

The group sullenly said yes, except for Aunt Gertie who wailed, "AHHHHHHH HOWARD."

Ms. Sweeney pushed open the accordion doors, Jamie looked away. The whole family moved into the viewing room, their mouths agape.

Mick Schmuk lay partially in the casket, face down, his legs dangling out. "What is this, some sorta sick joke?" asked Aunt Gertie.

Mrs. Sweeney couldn't believe her eyes, "Oh, sweet Jesus."

"I think you have some explaining to do, Ms. Sweeney," said one of Howard Hope's children.

Mrs. Sweeney was speechless. "I...I...I..."

"That's not dad," said Howard Jr. after giving the body a closer look.

That's when the patriarch, Howard Hope, made his appearance. His weight had unravelled the knots of the coats used to keep him in the closet. On cue, he fell forward. The doors of the closet burst open and he landed face first onto the floor.

Aunt Gertie, pushed herself away from the crowd, swatting away the hands that were trying to help support her. "It's a miracle. Howard climbed into the closet...Howard! Howard! Get up you dumb son of a bitch."

There was a dark and defeated silence.

"Ms. Sweeney, who put my father in the closet? I mean, corpses just can't climb into closets by themselves," said Howard Jr.

"And who the hell is the other person?" asked Howard Jr.'s wife.

Ms. Sweeney was close to tears. She was baffled by

the whole state of affairs. Her only thought, some funeral vandals had struck. Funeral vandals. What is the world coming to?

"This is the worst God damned funeral I have ever been to," spat Aunt Gertie. Then she narrowed her eyes on Ms. Sweeney, "I hope whoever is responsible will burn in hell for all eternity."

Ms. Sweeney collapsed into one of the folding chairs.

*****

While the Hope family focused its collective rage on Ms. Sweeney, Jamie quietly exited the funeral home. Once outside, he walked briskly past the Gipta Temporary Agency. He never once looked back. And then he started to run, a casual jog that slowly evolved into a frantic sprint. A mad dash. Jamie Dropping ran down South Normal Street, dodging pedestrians. Adam fleeing from Eden.

Some pedestrians felt Jamie Dropping brush past them. They couldn't understand what he was running from or where he was going. They were instinctively irritated by his hurry and bustle on such a humid summer day. There was no need to be in such a rush. After all, it was just a typical humdrum afternoon, the boredom of melting ice cream.

WALKING WALTER[1]

I soon found out there was a lot I didn't know about Jenny. To start with, she had a dog – a decrepit, poodley sort of dog with white fluffy fur and impossibly short legs. When I moved in, Jenny introduced me to the mutt. "Jamie, this is Walter," she beamed.

Walter looked stiff.

"Is he dead?"

"Of course not," Jenny huffed. But the dog didn't seem to be breathing. I nudged him with my foot. He cocked his head, made an effort to look around, and then collapsed.

After meeting Walter, I seldom saw him in motion. He

---

1 Originally published in Hodge Podge Issue 1, November 2008.

had probably been a real yappy, bouncy son of a bitch in his prime, but now his yapping and bouncing days were long gone.

During the day, Walter had as much energy as a pillow. He just lay around farting. But at night, Walter was an ass licking maniac. He would slurp and snort about his asshole from midnight to dawn. It was the type of noise that made me dream of driving my car off a cliff. It was horrifying.

Just when I had gotten used to Walter's behavior patterns – sleep all day and slurp all night – he did something that was completely out of character. One night, he came racing into the living room. He was possessed by some crazy energy and he bounded into the living room like Lassie whacked out on crack and tried to dig a hole in the floor.

"Look," I told Jenny, "Walter's digging his grave." Jenny didn't like me joking about Walter like that.

After that night, Walter pulled this little stunt every now and again. He would race into the living room, dig and dig and dig, and then slowly come to his senses. Walter was dying, but he wasn't stupid. He would quickly understand the impossibility of the hole, and he would limp away and collapse somewhere. Defeated, until the next shock of life would send him digging. Whenever Walter had one of these "panic attacks," (that's what Jenny called them) Jenny never tried to stop him – even when he ripped the carpet. She never said a word. She just watched him, her eyes heavy with tears.

Me, I found it ironic that Walter was digging his

grave in the living room.

I wasn't a pet person, and Walter really gave me the creeps. I had trouble with the name. What kind of person names a dog Walter? I couldn't understand why he had a person name. What was wrong with Spuds or Rover? A good old fashioned dog name. Did Jenny think he was human? Was she that stupid? Maybe she thought Walter was a cute name? What did the Walters' around the world think about their name being used for dogs? Damned Walter. Whenever Jenny talked about Walter, I couldn't remember if she was talking about a dog or some subnormal friend of hers.

"Walter's lost his appetite again."
-- or --
"Walter seems so happy with his new squeaky toy."
-- or --
"With his new diet, Walter isn't farting so much."

I did a little detective work and soon found out the secret behind the name. Jenny's father's name was Jason **W**. Pressbird. Good old **double-u**. Jason **Walter** Pressbird, I learned from Jenny, was a bit eccentric. He ran around saying things like, "I can hear goldfish farting." He was a real gem of a man. He died in his armchair when Jenny was 18. His last words were, "Don't gouge the God damned ice cream."

The fact that Jenny named the dog after her dead father was a clear sign that she needed a shrink. Maybe someday she'd want to name me Walter. The whole pet/dead father thing was giving off a Psycho vibe. Then it got worse.

One day, Jenny told me, "Since you're home all day, why don't you take Walter for a walk in the afternoon."

"Darling, just because I don't have a job doesn't mean I'm not busy."

"You'll need these," Jenny wasn't listening. She handed me some surgical gloves. She had a box stuffed with surgical gloves.

"What the hell are these for?"

"So you can pick up his business."

I began to feel faint.

"This way you can get to know Walter better."

"I'll get to know him better by handling his shit? The whole thing sounds a bit sick." Jenny had flipped out completely.

I looked at Walter. He was lying in the corner of the room like a sack of potatoes.

But Jenny wasn't kidding. She kissed me and whispered, "If you wanna get some, you gotta give some." Like everything in life, it all came down to sex. My will was weak. If sex meant surgical gloves and dog shit, so be it.

So, me and Walter went for walks.

Walter wasn't much of a walker anymore. He would hobble down the stairs of the apartment building and then stall. I would have to pick up the little bastard and carry him outside. I would plop him down in the grass and he would just stand there. His little dog brain was busy chasing its own tail.

I would drag him around the block, and he would try to piss on everything. He was marking his territory, and Walter believed that everything belonged to him. He had a bladder the size of a grape, and he would run out of piss pretty quick. But that didn't matter to Walter. Not Walter. He would go around pretending to piss on car tires. He would raise one of his tiny hind legs and try to squeeze out a drop or two. He really enjoyed pissing on car tires.

Sometimes he would piss on a car tire and then waddle into his own puddle and stick his nose in it and get a good nose full. I was convinced that he could stand there sniffing his piss for hours. Sometimes cars would come down the street and Walter would be wading in his own puddle of piss in the road. I would let out his leash a little. Give him a little running room. Walter never budged and the cars always missed him. They would swerve at the last minute and the drivers would scream out, "HEY ASSHOLE, GET YOUR DOG OUTA THE ROAD." These walks with Walter convinced me that the world was crammed full of idiots and assholes.

Every afternoon we did the same route. And every afternoon our fifteen minute walk was like a stroll through hell. I would yank Walter this way and that way, watch him stagger around in his puddles of piss, pick up little piles of poop, and the walk always ended with me rabid and cursing, carrying him home.

After a couple weeks of walking Walter, the whole ordeal was killing me. Plus, Jenny had been less than sincere in her offer of "getting some." At night, she was always too tired, or her head hurt, or she had cramps, or she just wanted to watch TV, or she needed to do some work, or she wasn't in the mood, or her feet ached. There was always something wrong.

Whenever she would give me one of her lackluster excuses, I would moan, "But I'm walking Walter."

"I know. You're a good boy." She talked to me like I was a dog. "Tomorrow, OK?" then she would yawn, roll over and fall asleep.

On the last day I walked Walter, we were returning home and he made a stop in our neighbor's yard. He liked to shit in our neighbor's yard. Every afternoon he took a shit in that yard. And me, I would be there with my surgical gloves and a plastic bag, like some two-bit detective collecting evidence.

On that particular day, the neighbor was out. He was an old, unhappy guy, with a white t-shirt, baggy blue shorts and black socks that he had pulled up to his thighs. He had a sour pucker of a face. He was standing in the middle of his yard with his hose, watering some dead plants. He saw me and Walter, and hobbled over with the hose. "Hey you."

"What?"

"How come you bring your dog to my yard all the time?"

"I always pick up his business," I held up my hands so he could see my surgical gloves.

"Why don't you take him across the street? Will you get lost if you cross the street?"

"Why don't you go back inside and die, you old bag of shit."

The old geezer didn't say anything. He pointed his hose at me and squeezed the trigger.

I was soaked, and Walter was pushing out a fresh one. I picked it up and chucked it at the old man's house.

"FUCK YOU," I yelled

The old man squirted me in the face, my glasses went flying. I bent over to pick them up, and he squirted me in the ass. He was having a good time with his hose.

"I'm gonna shove that hose up your..." He squirted me again and I ran off dragging Walter all the way home, up the stairs and into the apartment.

That was it. Jenny was going to have to face the facts: Walter had outlived his planned doggy obsolescence, and I was done walking the little bastard. "Either Walter goes or I go," I howled but there was no one there to hear it. I was soaking and paced back and forth with crazy energy. I cursed Walter. I cursed Jenny. I cursed my mother and father's procreating urge, I cursed my floundering existence.

After all my cursing and pacing, I dried myself off and waited for Jenny. "Either Walter goes or I go," I decreed again, with a little less passion. The storm of my fury was weakening. I knew that given the choice of me or Walter, she would choose the damn dog. So, I needed to come up with plan-b.

Later, when Jenny came home from work, I greeted her at the door.

"How was your day, honey?"

"Crappy," she kicked off her shoes.

"Mine too. I was attacked by the neighbor."

"What?"

"No big deal, but maybe we should talk about Walter." I tried to be as euphemistic as possible, "Do you think that it might be a good idea to put Walter down?"

"What?"

"Maybe it's the humane thing to do, I mean look at him."

Walter was inert as usual.

Jenny went inside the bedroom and slammed the door.

I knocked. "Jenny, sweetheart. I'm just thinking of Walter. He seems to be suffering so much."

Walter farted.

Jenny didn't say anything. She was too busy pitching my clothes out the bedroom window.

THE FIRST TIME

Prior to watching illegal access pornography, sixteen year old Jamie Dropping hadn't given much creative thought to the enterprise of sex. It was usually a sloppy thirty second fantasy featuring sexed up sitcom characters like Laverne and Shirley. Jamie played the role of Carmine, The Big Ragu. He would usually show up unannounced while the girls were taking showers or lounging in their negligee. They would seduce him and before he knew it the whole affair was over. Laverne and Shirley would float him a kiss as he morphed back into Jamie Dropping, laying on his soiled sheets hounded by guilt for masturbating.

*****

The word *masturbation* was such an ugly word. It led a miserable linguistic existence. As far as words went, it was a lonely, friendless word. Perhaps not as lonely as words like castration and emasculation, but still not a word that you would willingly hang out with.

Jamie considered that the problem with masturbating wasn't the act, it was actually the word. He believed that by calling it something else, he would actually feel less guilty about it. He baptized masturbation *selfebration* (self + celebration = selfebration) which Jamie typically pronounced much like *selfabrasion*. Regardless, his nocturnal practice of *selfebration* or *selfabrasion* still seemed like masturbation.

*****

One night, as the TV yawned images of late night talk shows, everything changed. His parents had gone to bed, and as Jamie flipped through the channels, he stumbled onto an image. For only a split second, he saw what looked like a piece of cinnamon toast being buttered. Jamie found the image strangely arousing, but because his parents didn't subscribe to the channel, he had to suffer the scrambled, scrolling images. He watched and watched and he soon realized that the cinnamon toast was a vagina and it was not really being buttered at all. Jamie Dropping was struck by lightning. The lightbulb in his groin buzzed with light. *Oh, brave new world.*

From that night on, Jamie would wait impatiently for his parents to trod off to bed so that he could sit and watch the broken, dissected and surreal images of black and white and sometime greenish men and women engaged in the great act of fornication. It was like watching a porno painted by Picasso.

Once his parents were snoring, he muted the TV and watched. The whole living room was filled with a flashing silence as Jamie Dropping devoured the images of men and women in broken scrolling ecstasy.

*****

With the help of the porno channel, Jamie began to feel less conflicted about *selfabrasion or selfebration*. He realized that that's what these shows were all about. They wanted people everywhere to *selfabrade (selfebrate)*. And there were people that paid to watch this channel so that they could discretely do *it* in the comfort of their own living rooms. Suddenly, Jamie didn't feel so lonely anymore. There were probably millions of other people just like him, *selfabrading (selfebrating)* all over the world.

Just as Jamie was beginning to feel comfortable with *selfebrasion*, something truly awful happened. One night he turned on the channel and watched 20 minutes of the Marx Brothers' *Duck Soup,* fully erect, before he realized that it really was Groucho Marx and not some sort of Marx Brothers sex fantasy show. *Duck Soup* marked the beginning of the end. The following night, after 5 minutes he realized that the movie was *Casablanca*.

Night after night he would turn on the channel hoping for a flash flood, a riot, of fornication. But instead, he would find the slapstick of the Three Stooges, Laurel and Hardy, the Marx Brothers, Buster Keaton, Charlie Chaplin, Fatty Arbuckle... Jamie took it personally, the channel was making fun of him. It mocked him.

On Jamie's last night of viewing, the title of the show bounced all over the screen, Jamie's heart quickened, his mouth went dry, the hair on his arms stood straight up, he felt a stirring in his groin; but the title lingered long enough for him to realize that the show was called *Fatty Gets Ahead* not *Fatty Gets Head*. His disappointment was profound. He sighed a sigh of defeat, switched the channel, turned up the volume. A jolt of canned laughter boomed from the television.

*****

The porno channel had been Jamie's sexual wake up call. But it was also more than that. It had hijacked him, taken him for a joyride and then ditched him in the abandoned lot of his ordinary life. He had been taken hostage, released again only to realize that the world was the same but he had changed. He was no longer the same person. Everything had changed. The thrill of *selfabrading* was gone. The titillation was dead.

*****

One day at school, as Jamie was walking down the hallway to his algebra class, he tripped or perhaps someone tripped him. It doesn't really matter. What is important is this: Jamie fell and his algebra book landed at *her* feet. She was new to the school and her name was Molly. But Jamie Dropping did not know that yet. He stood up and saw *her* for the first time. All of mathematical evolution existed for this sole purpose, this single flake of time. An algebra book flung into the void and landing at Molly's feet.

Jamie had never seen anything like her: the linear

equation of her gaze, the delicate curve of her smile, the ripe geometry of her body. Usually, the other sex intimidated Jamie. Girls troubled him in the same way that failing biology troubled him: the female form – an irritated red *F* scribbled across his soul. But there was something different about Molly. It wasn't just how she looked but *how* she looked at him. She hadn't been at the school long enough to know that his social standing oscillated between loser and geek.

She picked up his algebra book and handed it to him. "I think you dropped this," she said and walked away. Even her voice was a miracle of sound.

Jamie hugged his algebra book to his chest, his heart pounding.

*****

After that brief yet momentous encounter, Jamie Dropping couldn't stop thinking about Molly. She was everywhere. As he did his homework, her voice echoed brightly through his mind, *"I think you dropped this...dropped this....dropped this..."* While the TV announced the evening news of murders, hurricanes, floods, corruption, debt, the end of the world, she would suddenly appear in the hallway, dressed in sexy lingerie, a corset perhaps, smiling at him ambiguously or offering him a glass of freshly squeezed orange juice.

As the days passed, he did nothing but lay around the house like an injured animal, sighing and thinking about Molly. He began to fancy himself a poet and he wrote her love poems.

...My heart is a plucked bird singing inside my chest...

...Your name is a burning doughnut in my mind...

...You are an arson and have set my soggy cereal mind on fire...

He wrote about plucked birds, fire and soggy cereal.

At school Jamie spent his free time spying on Molly. He would watch her secretly, lingering at the water fountain near her locker, taking long drinks of water between classes. He couldn't bring himself to speak to her though, because he had no idea what to say. The words that expressed how he felt about her had not been invented yet. He also noticed that as he came closer to her, words that had been invented also seemed impossible to use. So he resigned to simply watch her from the water fountain, wrestling with the tremendous urge to urinate.

*****

Then one day, Molly spoke to him. She sidled up to his locker and enquired, "Did you finish your algebra homework?"

His heart pounded furiously in his chest. He dropped the books that he was holding, papers flooded out his folders and scattered across the floor. "Of course," the words exploded from Jamie's mouth.

There was an awkward pause.

"Do you think I could copy it?"

"Oh, yeah, sure," said Jamie. He rummaged through the papers that covered the floor searching for his homework. He gave it to her and he watched Molly copy his answers. He fell in love with her slender fingers and her teeth marked pencil, with its overused eraser. He fell in love with the speed at which she copied his answers. He was happy that she was mathematically challenged or perhaps just a bit lazy. It didn't matter. Being used made him feel useful.

She handed him back his paper, "Thanks. I'll see you in class," smiled and then walked away.

*****

The next day, Jamie waited around hoping that Molly would arrive at his locker again. He hoped she would need to copy his assignment. He had prepared answers with care, changing all the x's to m's and all the y's to j's. It wasn't merely homework. It was a love letter. She would understand the subtlety of his quadratic equations.

Molly showed up, and Jamie spoke to her as she copied.

"So do you like it here?"

"It's OK."

"Yeah, it's not too bad."

Silence.

"Where did you go before?"

"Sommerset..."

"That's a pretty good school. Why did you leave?"

"Is this an j or a y?"

Jamie didn't need to look at his paper. He knew it was a j. "That's a j," he blushed. He was in love for the first time in his life.

*****

Jamie didn't remember how or when it had happened, but at some point in his past he and Howard Strangula had become friends. For Jamie, it was a dubious and difficult friendship. It was sometimes hard for Jamie to tolerate Howard and his incessant ego babble. Howard liked talking about little other than himself and, for Jamie, every lunch hour was a nauseating inventory of Howard's greatness. Like the time he saved the child from the runaway roller coaster (why wasn't it in the newspaper? Howard had no idea why this event wasn't news worthy. He had even been interviewed by a flock of reporters) or the time he had sex with the Cindy Crawford look alike. It was a wild pack of hungry lies.

Because he was a liar he was always regarded by his classmates, even Jamie, with careful suspicion. Howard always seemed guilty of something. He lurked through the hallway, hid behind his books during class. He always seemed to be privately plotting some war against truth. Perhaps his fellow students felt this way because his smile looked more like a sneer than a smile, perhaps it was because of his questionable limp or perhaps it was because his face was pock marked with ulterior motives. Whatever the reason, he was well on his way to win the unsavory honor of being voted *The most likely to start World War III* by his classmates.

Besides the sneering smile and the acne; he also had small jealous eyes. And with those beady eyes he had spied on Jamie who was spying on Molly. He had seen it all. Jamie at the water fountain, taking long drinks of water. Jamie watching Molly over the top of his algebra text book. He had seen Jamie's secret smiles and he had seen Jamie lapse into a daydream in the middle of a sentence. Staring off into space, a dopey smile smeared across his face. Howard didn't like what he saw. Jamie's starry eyed happiness made him unhappy.

Being Jamie's best friend, he had no other choice but to teach him a very important lesson. Love was a pile of shit. So, one day after he watched Jamie giggling in the hallway while Molly was copying his algebra homework he decided he had had enough. After school he told Jamie, "So are you gonna ask that Molly chick out?"

Rejection terrified Jamie. "I'm not up to it. I mean, I'm not emotionally capable of asking her out."

"What the hell does that mean? Emotionally capable. Sounds to me like you're a pussy."

Jamie was offended. He was a bit delicate, but he was no pussy.

"I'm just not ready to ask her out. Do you think she likes me?"

"No."

"Why not?"

"Dude, she's just using you."

"She's not using me. She's just a bit lazy."

"Dude, listen to me, she's got no respect for you. You're just some algebra geek who has all the right answers. She doesn't look at you as a man. Look at Blane Dongle. All the girls like that son of a bitch. They respect him."

"I don't know what you mean."

"It's easy. All the chicks know he's got a dick. But

you, they aren't so sure. Do you remember the movie *The Full Monty?* Everyone thought those guys were a bunch of dickless losers. They had to show everyone that they still had dicks, so that's why they did the whole strip tease bullshit. It was about showing their wives and ex-wives that they still had balls."

Jamie was irritated with Howard's reasoning. He didn't understand why Howard couldn't believe that Molly found him attractive. Jamie reasoned aloud, "There are 38 people in our algebra class. Why did she choose me? Why not one of the other guys? Did you ever think that maybe she just likes me?"

"No offense, dude, but have you taken a look at yourself in the mirror lately."

Jamie tried hard not to look at himself in the mirror. He hated the way he looked: the acne that encircled his mouth, his glasses, the tufts of facial hair on his neck and cheeks, his bulbous and greasy nose. But most of all he hated his hair, his monotonous hairstyle. It lacked ambition or pep – parted in the middle, brushed back. Feathered. He looked like a loser version of Ralph Macchio from the *Karate Kid.*

"You need to show Molly that you have balls."

"How?"

Howard smiled. He had not been prepared for the direction the conversation had taken, but he beamed deliciously at the path they were on.

*****

Outside the boys locker room, Jamie endured a full blown panic attack while Howard explained the plan for the fifth time.

It was simple, at least that was how Howard described it. But Jamie didn't find it simple. Plus there were parts of the plan that he abhorred. One such part was buying a condom from Blane Dongle. Another part that was equally terrifying was going on a date with Howard's cousin, who had the unfortunate name, Helga. Every time that Howard explained the plan to Jamie, he would fade out when Helga was introduced.

"I don't understand why I need to go on a date with your cousin."

"Dude, I told you a million fucking times. When you buy the condom from Dongle, he'll tell everyone. Word will get round to Molly. Then you nail my cousin Helga."

Jamie breathed in through his nose and exhaled through his mouth with his eyes closed.

"Remember *The Full Monty*. You need to get your dick some publicity."

"Oh God," sighed Jamie.

"So are you ready to do this?" Howard was losing his patience.

"Not really..."

"Don't worry, I'll do the talking."

Howard pushed open the door to the locker room. Blane Dongle, half barbarian half idiot, whose sole purpose of his jock strap existence was to terrorize the underclassmen, was putting on his socks.

Blane Dongle was Herculean in all dimensions except reasoning. He was a demolition of human muscle, with the intellect of a nursery school potty.

"Hey, Dongle we heard you got some condoms to sell."

Blane stopped pulling up his socks and took a good look at Howard and Jamie. He turned his massive head slowly. His voice was as loud as a thunderstorm, "Whoo dolt you I sell condims?"

Howard looked at Jamie. Jamie looked at the ground.

"I heard some guys talking in the parking lot."

"Wy don you go by sim from da sore?"

There was a slight pause. Then Howard said, "He can't buy them from a store because he suffers from acute agoraphobia."

Blane reminisced sadly, "Me dad bonded wit sheeps on his farm afer long drinkin nights when da mind play tricks on da senses."

Not sure what Blane's father's bonding with sheep had to do with anything, Howard clarified, "He's afraid of shopping centers."

Jamie was beginning to feel like an inanimate object. Blane and Howard's conversation about him made him feel as though he didn't exist. He felt he needed to make his presence felt, and he also needed to defend himself. Jamie wheezed, "I'm going to nail his cousin."

Howard rolled his eyes in disappointment.

Blane chuckled and drooled a bit on himself, "Yeah? Wats he name?"

"What?" asked Jamie timidly.

"Very funny Blane. That's just the type of comment we would expect from a homophobe like you."

Blane slowly rose to his feet. He was a giant.

Enormous. His thigh was as thick as Jamie's body. "You kallin me a homo?"

Jamie hid behind Howard. "I didn't call you a homo Blane. I'm sorry. He just wants to buy a condom."

Blane pulled a condom from his wallet and threw it at Howard. "Tin bucks."

Howard nudged Jamie. Jamie pulled out a ten dollar bill and handed it over to Blane.

*****

On the drive to Helga's house, Jamie was so nervous that his stomach was doing somersaults. His hands were wet with sweat, and he had such trouble breathing that he nearly fainted twice. He couldn't believe that he had let Howard coach him into this mess.

Howard had told Jamie that Helga looked exactly like Cindy Crawford. Jamie was certain with a name like Helga she was not going to be pretty in any sense of the word. He imagined a nerdy, subnormal, cockeyed girl with braces. With a name like Helga he was convinced that she probably didn't bathe regularly.

As he pulled up in front of her house, he saw Helga sitting on the porch. He wasn't pleasantly surprised. She was dressed in nearly all the colors of the rainbow. She had a pink purse and boots, a red shirt, orange pants and green button up sweater.

She pulled open the car door and slumped into the passenger seat. Jamie smiled and stuttered, "He...Hell...Hello, I'm Jamie."

She looked Jamie and said, "No shit sherlock."

*****

Howard's description of his cousin was a bit over exaggerated. The only resemblance between Helga and Cindy Crawford was a mole. Whereas Cindy Crawford's mole was actually considered a beauty mark, a blemish that only made her more beautiful, Helga's mole, which stared at you from the end of her nose, underlined her ugliness.

She had a Bride of Frankenstein beehive-ish hairdo. Her mouth was full of uneven teeth covered in the barbed wire of her braces, and her complexion lurked like a convict somewhere between the grey of solitary confinement and the pale white of the morgue.

*****

The date began with dinner. Jamie took Helga to a restaurant that he had always liked: Tony's Bigtime Steakhouse. The restaurant was owned and managed by Tony Malarky. Before becoming a restaurateur, Tony Malarky was better known as The Mauler, the arch enemy of Bulldog Riptide and one time Transatlantic Wresting Federation Champion of the World.

Jamie pulled into the parking lot. Helga read the sign aloud, "Tony's Bigtime Steakhouse. We feed your family death."

Once upon a time, Tony's Bigtime Steakhouse proudly boasted, "We feed your family the best." Although there were those who criticized Tony's slogan, claiming that it didn't express a complete thought, Tony didn't care. It didn't matter if you ordered an omelet, a burger, a steak, it was going to be the best. Of course, Tony's best was slightly below average.

Unfortunately though, some young punk, most likely Howard Strangula, had defaced his sign and had violated the slogan of the Tony's Bigtime Steakhouse. The sign no longer boasted "We feed your family the best" but lugubriously sneered, "We feed your family death."

"It used to say We feed your family the best. But some kids vandalized the sign."

"Hmmm," said Helga, "It looks like a hang out for cheapskates."

Jamie was slightly offended. It wasn't an expensive restaurant, sure, but it was worthy of their first date. "The food is good, though."

Helga had her doubts.

Inside the restaurant the young couple was escorted by an unhappy waitress to a booth.

Tony's Bigtime Steakhouse, besides being a restaurant, was also a museum dedicated to The Mauler's professional wresting career. On the walls hung photographs of Tony in his peak. Other wrestling artifacts were also on display: his skimpy shorts, his boots, his various glittering robes. In the booth where Jamie and Helga sat, Tony was pictured standing on the ropes poised to attack, blood dripped from his gashed forehead. His face was locked in a horrible savage grimace.

The waitress arrived and said nothing.

Jamie said, "I'll have the The Mauler Burger and a Pepsi."

Helga studied the menu. She had left the burgers and had ventured into the steaks. She wasn't reading the name of the food, she was looking at the prices. She found a steak for $18.50 "I'll take the The Super Mauler Ribeye steak."

"Salad or soup?"

"Salad."

Jamie panicked. The steaks were always expensive. He quickly scanned the menu for the Super Mauler Ribeye. But before he could find it, the waitress yanked the menu from him.

The rest of the meal was suffered in silence. Helga was insulted she had been brought to a dump like Tony's Bigtime Steakhouse and Jamie was calculating over and over again various different dessert scenarios that Helga could possibly order to determine if he could afford the rest of the night.

*****

Howard had instructed Jamie to take his cousin to the movies. "But take her to a foreign film. A French or Italian movie. Because those types of movies have lots of nudity and this would get her in the mood." That was Howard's advice.   Jamie had found the instructions a bit strange. Howard seemed to know too much about his cousin's sexual turn-ons. Regardless, Jamie did as he was told and he found one of the artsy-fartsy theaters downtown was showing an Italian movie called *Umberto D.*

At the theater, Helga seemed to perk up a bit. "A foreign film," she purred. She even took Jamie by the arm which made him blush and feel strangely uncomfortable. He tried to inconspicuously wriggle his arm free, but Helga clung on to him tightly.

The theater was empty except for a lone man, in a

tweed jacket with long grey sideburns. An extinguished pipe was locked in his teeth.

"Do you know what this movie is about?" asked Helga loudly.

"No," whispered Jamie.

Then Helga turned to the man in tweed. "Hey mister, what's this movie about?"

"It's about an old man and his dog," snapped the man.

"Are there any good sex scenes. Because my boyfriend and me like hot sexy movies."

Jamie sank into his seat. He wasn't completely comfortable graduating to the rank of Helga's boyfriend. It was as if the weight of the word *boyfriend* was pushing him down. Crushing him. He could feel the glare of the tweed wearing man on the back of his head.

"Unless you think a movie about an old man trying to find someone to take care of a dog so that he can go die sexy; I suggest you go down the street and watch *Debbie Does Dallas*," retaliated the man with scowl.

Helga turned away from the man and glared at Jamie.

Jamie smiled and whispered reassuringly, "I'm sure there's going to be a sex scene or two."

"There'd better be," said Helga.

*****

There were no sex scenes. At least there were no sex scenes during the first twenty minutes. That's all that Jamie and Helga were able to see. Once the movie started, Helga would sigh loudly and then say something

~65~

like, "Oh my God, this is so crappy" or "Dear Christ in heaven, this is stupidest piece of shit ever made."

The man wearing tweed at first, hissed "SSSSSHHHHH." Helga ignored the man and continued to comment loudly. The hisses became more violent. But Helga didn't stop. Finally, he left the theater. Helga, seeing the light spill into the theater from the open door, said, "Thank God that hissing son of a bitch left."

Then the door opened again and the man in tweed was escorted by an usher.

"This little idiot and his girlfriend have no respect for Italian neo-realism. They haven't stopped talking since the film began."

"The movie's in Italian. You can't even understand what the hell they are saying."

"I can't read the subtitles with all your gabbing."

"I'm going to have to ask you two to leave," said the usher.

Helga jumped to her feet, and spat, "I don't want to watch another minute of this stupid piece of shit anyway."

She marched out of the theater and Jamie scampered out behind her.

*****

Jamie was sure that the date was over after they had been kicked out of the theater, which he wasn't too unhappy about. Helga was furious, "So let me get this straight. That was really a movie about some old fucker trying to find some asshole to take care of his dog so that he can go kill himself?"

Jamie began to apologize, "I didn't know what the

movie was about..."

Helga didn't listen. "Maybe he was so fucking depressed because he went on a date with you."

Helga recoiled into full sulk. She seemed really pissed off, and she summarized the date, "You took me to a restaurant owned by a wrestler and then took me to a movie about a man and stupid dog. I'm glad we were kicked out. Because I would have been bored to death if we stayed a minute longer." The date was over. Jamie's first date. A complete failure. Jamie was driving home in uncomfortable silence when she suddenly said, "Pull into that parking lot here."

"Why?"

"Because I need to take a piss."

Jamie did as he was told. He pulled into the parking lot of an office building that was closed.

****

Helga had been insincere about her need to urinate. As the car rolled to stop in front of a large green garbage dumpster, she had climbed into the backseat of the car.

"So, my cousin said that you're a real stud," she said doubtfully.

In his fantasies with Laverne and Shirley Jamie was more than a stud. He was *the* Big Ragu. But in reality Jamie knew that he was not stud material. All the porno movies he had watched had convinced him that he was vastly inadequate. The men in those movies had anacondas between their legs. Jamie had a bookworm between his legs.

Helga began peeling off some of her colors, starting

with the green sweater. Just before she pulled off her orange shirt, she whispered, "Why don't you join me back here?"

Jamie sighed and was about to tell Helga that he didn't think it was a good idea when Howard's voice boomed in his mind, "You need to get your dick publicity. Think of Molly. Think of *The Full Monty*."

Jamie got out of the car and tried to open the backseat door. It was locked. He opened the driver's door, pressed the unlock button, he pulled open the door and sat down on the edge of the seat. He folded his hands on his lap and watched Helga with his mouth slightly open, giving him the appearance of a choir boy of subnormal intelligence.

Helga's shirt had been removed exposing a white bra, and she unbuckled her pants and smiled a fractured grey smile.

*****

Jamie did not find Helga attractive, but being so close to female flesh made him feel the same way that Columbus most likely felt when he first caught a glimpse of the New World: lucky. Jamie was also surprised. The date had gone so bad, and now Helga was naked in the backseat of the car. She was what the boys at school labelled as "easy." But what Jamie and the other boys at school didn't know about Helga was that she had a cheerleader's enthusiasm about sex. It was something that instinctively made her want to jump up and down, do cartwheels and backflips. She longed for sex, but she was sadly disappointed that the boys she fantasized about screwing didn't share that same desire to explore sex with her. So she had to tolerate boys like Jamie Dropping. She tolerated them like a bad rash, always hoping to find the one that would light her metaphorical fire.

Helga had peeled off her panties and unclasped her bra. She was completely naked, stripped down to her most primitive and basic beauty. Jamie's heart did jumping jacks in his chest.

Helga didn't waste any time. She attacked. She slid her tongue into his mouth – probing his molars. Jamie, eyes wide open, was a bit terrified. He had no idea what to do. Sure, he had rehearsed intercourse nearly a thousand lonely and sticky nights with his sexed up versions of Laverne and Shirley, but that was fiction. Fantasy. Here he was confronted by the real thing: Helga's hot stale breath, the metal of her braces.

Then Helga lay down and pulled Jamie on top of her. He drooled into her mouth. Her tongue flicked in and out of his. His hand accidentally slid across one of her breasts and she moaned. She yanked Jamie up and down on top of her, Jamie looked into her eyes. They were wild with pleasure.

She whispered hotly, "Take off your pants."

Jamie did as he was told, but with great reservation. He thought about the men from the movies. Exposing himself like this, becoming naked, was not easy. Helga was impatient. She started pulling and yanking at the legs of his pants. Once depantsed, Helga saw his penis standing at attention. She ordered, "Give me the condom."

Jamie handed it to her.

She tore the envelope open with her teeth. Then she rolled it slowly onto his penis. She kissed him viciously, biting his lower lip. Jamie came immediately. Helga had no idea what had happened. She lay down and invited Jamie, "Come and ride the tiger." Jamie sat, dumfounded, his mouth hung open, staring at his penis.

*****

Jamie lay on top of Helga and poked and poked at her vagina with his penis. He was trying to throw a bulls eye blindfolded. She helped him find the spot. "Uhhhh," she grunted as he entered.

Helga pushed and pulled Jamie. Back and forth, back and forth. With every movement the backseat of the car would let out a dreary and dismal squeal. It was the type of sound that whale would make before it died, and it was unbearably loud.

He continued the *fort-da* game of in-and-out, and Helga lay underneath him with her eyes closed. Jamie stared into her silver mouth and saw bits of the Mauler's ribeye stuck in her braces. Between the squeaking, Helga's mouth, and the disappointment of premature ejaculation he began to lose his focus. Soon, nothing was happening. It was merely motion without substance. He felt that he was going limp, and he began to worry about the condom sliding off his penis.

*****

"Whisper sexy stuff to me," sighed Helga.

"Like what?"

"You know, like the stuff from the movies."

Jamie had always watched those types of movies muted. Even if he had turned the volume on, he only heard the sound of static. So, he improvised, "I think you're...sexy...like...a glamour model...not a high fashion model...who are usually too skinny..."

"What?"

The car squeaked and squawked with every movement.

"You're sexier than...that woman with...what's her name...from the movie..."

"Never mind. Don't say anything."

Shortly after, his soldier slid out of her cave. Jamie tried hard to insert himself again. It was no use. It was like trying to pick a lock with an over boiled spaghetti noodle. He sat up and half smiled. He didn't know what else to say or do.

*****

Jamie had thought that sex would be like a wild storm – flashes of lightning, booming thunder and rain, lots of rain. But the storm of the night had turned out to be a mere drizzle, and a short one at that. Helga sat up and pouted, "That was it?"

Just when Jamie thought it couldn't get any worse there was a loud knocking on the driver side window.

Through the window fogged with steam, a featureless face blurted out, "Hey kid, put your pants on and move your car so we can do our job."

Jamie's heart pounded and his knees trembled. The disaster of the night was ending like the low budget horror film: secluded parking lot, naked kids in car, psychopath at window.

"Wh...who are you?" Jamie stuttered.

"Mr. Rubbish. Come on kid, you've parked in front of the God damned dumpster. Just go screw your girlfriend somewhere else."

"I'm not his girlfriend," shouted Helga.

Jamie sighed, pulled on his pants, climbed into the driver seat and drove away, the tires squealing.

*****

As they drove in silence, Jamie was lost in feelings of failure, and he began to wonder if he technically had lost his virginity. He concluded after five miles of reasoning, that he should've ejaculated inside Helga, otherwise it wasn't much different than masturbation. He conjectured that he had lost 50% of his virginity, and that made him feel even worse. He was an enormous loser. This was not the publicity his penis needed. And every now and then, Helga would add some extra punctuation to Jamie's dark contemplations, "That was the worst."

Jamie wasn't sure which part of the date was worse than the other. But he brooded about the sex and Helga's disgust after the sex. It had been a disaster. Even the usual peace and quiet of his mind was replaced with disaster. There was a riot of questions (why had he listened to Howard? Why didn't he tell Howard 'No'? Why didn't he think for himself? Why was he such a pushover? What was wrong with him?) In his mind, a mob hurtled stones and molotov cocktails, the police fired teargas. Everything was aflame. Burning.

Soon, they arrived at Helga's house. The front door was open and a bitter yellow light spilled out of the house and onto the dark lawn. Without a word, Helga launched herself out of the car and marched up to her house. Jamie wanted to say something, but he had no idea what.

*****

As he left the subdivision, he knew he had blown it. His own private Full Monty had been a failure. *The Full Monty* had ended with the men liberated from their sexual inadequacies and burdens. They were heroes and given a standing ovation. Jamie felt as though he was being booed out of town.

He drove around aimlessly. He was only sixteen years old, and he was already sexually frustrated. His thoughts instinctively drifted to girls: lingerie models, music video stars, anchor women, the cheerleaders of the Dallas Cowboys, movie stars... He thought about Molly. He sighed her name.

He began to dissect himself at some point as he

drove: why was he the way he was? Why was he afraid of talking to Molly? He came to the conclusion that he had not been sexually liberated. He was bound and chained by his inhibitions. Jamie was both obsessed and troubled by sex. Although he never stopped thinking about it, he always felt that sex was something to be kept secret – at least it wasn't something you wanted to advertise to the adult world. He even felt guilty for wanting to have sex with someone other than himself, although he was also plagued with guilt for masturbating. He wasn't sure why he felt this way, but he instinctively blamed his parents for his sexual hang-ups. Sex made him feel filthy, like a pervert. Sex scared him. The other sex frightened him. This is why he didn't talk to Molly.

****

Jamie decided that the night wasn't over. He could still end it heroically. Sure, the standing ovation was out of the question, but there was still a chance for redemption. He could still overcome his fears. His Full Monty wasn't over yet. He pulled into the parking lot of Meijers grocery store.

He was resolute in mission. He quickly strolled into the pharmacy section and found, nestled between the toothpaste and the hair styling gel, a vast and overwhelming selection of condoms. Jamie had never imagined that there were so many different brands and types. He wanted to make an informed decision, choosing the best condom for his penis, but he also wanted to get the hell out of there before anyone he knew would spot him gawking. He randomly picked up a pack of Trojans, and then he decided that he needed to purchase something else. Something that would camouflage the condoms. Something that would make the transaction seem less sexually promiscuous. Jamie had wandered into the produce section and he grabbed the first item he saw: a five pound bag of Idaho potatoes. He then made his way to the checkout with his items.

It was late and there were only two lanes open. A young motherly looking woman was working lane number 3, and an elderly, grey haired man was working lane number 5. Jamie studied the old guy. He seemed like the type who had served in a foreign war, perhaps World War Two. Jamie imagined that the old guy had probably lost his virginity in some European brothel. He took lane number 5.

He put the potatoes and the condoms on the counter. The old guy grunted out a hello and then scanned the potatoes. He looked at the box of condoms and then he looked at Jamie.

"Are those yours son?"

Jamie looked away and whispered, "Yes."

"Hmmm," said the old guy. "Do you know that I never used a condom in my whole life?"

Oh, Christ, thought Jamie. He could feel himself

blushing. The last thing he wanted was to talk to some old fart at the grocery store about condoms.

"Do you know why I never used a condom?"

"You're sterile?"

"No, son. Because I never worried about the consequences. Do you know what I mean?"

Jamie couldn't understand why the old man needed to philosophize with him about his condom wearing habits. He wondered why the universe conspired against him.

The old guy picked up the condoms and placed them in a basket at the cash register for non purchased items. "You don't need any condoms, now do you son?"

Jamie wiped the sweat from his forehead, "No?" He couldn't believe what a prude the old fart was.

"Do you still want the potatoes?"

"Of course." Jamie needed the potatoes. They were the moral anchor of the transaction. The night may have been a failure, and Jamie may have only lost 50% of his virginity, but he would not be denied the potatoes.

*****

The next day at school, Jamie was sure he would be ridiculed and laughed at. He would be mocked and humiliated. As his mother drove him to school, he stared out the window and daydreamed, and his daydreams were horrific: kids singing "Like A Virgin" to him in the hallway amidst a chorus of laughter; his algebra teacher morphing into the old man from the super market and asking with an ironic wink, "Do you really need a condom, son?"; Molly doubling over with laughter and as she straightened up again her mouth had transformed into Helga's appalling silver mouth; finding a sign taped to his locker with the words "Premature Ejectulation" written on it. Jamie had such contempt for his tormentors that he even imagined they wouldn't be able to correctly spell the word *ejaculation*. By the time he had arrived at school, all the worrying about what the other kids would say about him had made him nauseous.

But to his surprise, all the worrying seemed to be pointless. No one was talking about him. Everyone seemed preoccupied with their high school dilemmas. There wasn't one whisper that included his name. No one, including Molly, seemed to even notice him.

Jamie was relieved. He was happy that no one said anything, but at the same time he wondered whether the silence was even worse than the humiliation. Silence meant that he wasn't even significant to be talked about. He may have been gossip proof, but that was because he was a mere cockroach in the social structure of high school. The only person that said anything was Howard. He asked with a leer, "So how was operation Full Monty?"

Jamie was an awful liar, but he tried anyway, "Great." Howard obviously hadn't spoken to Helga.

"Great? So tell me about it."

Jamie didn't have the courage to revisit the memory of the night. As a matter of fact, he was trying hard to suppress the memory, to forget that the whole night had happened.

Jamie thought about telling Howard what he wanted to hear, but he decided to be somewhat elusive, "Do you think it's possible just to lose 50% of your virginity?"

Howard's reaction puzzled Jamie. He smirked and then patted Jamie on the shoulder. He walked away whistling.

*****

Jamie spent the rest of the day beetling from classroom to classroom, enjoying the shade of his non existence.

BARBECUED

The relationship with my father-in-law could be described as *quiet*. We didn't have much to say to each other. One of the first times he had actually spoken to me was one muggy summer night, before Jenny and I tied the knot. It was one of those whiskey sipping man-to-man talks. We were sitting on the porch, swatting mosquitoes, watching the fireflies in the moonlight. Jenny and her mom were inside chatting about the wedding. My soon to be father-in-law asked, "Why don't you two slow down? Take a year off from one another and then see where you stand?"

I sipped my whiskey and didn't say anything. It was clear that he didn't want me for a son-in-law. I thought the best policy was a smile and silence – to remain mysteriously aloof. So that's what I did. I smiled and sipped my whiskey.

Anyway, who the hell was he to tell me what to do with Jenny? He wasn't even her real father. He was just a step-dad. I ignored his advice; Jenny and I got married, and the next thing I knew she was inviting them over every weekend. They came for supper, to watch *M.A.S.H.* reruns, to play euchre and Monopoly.

Their visits were worse than hell. I just wanted to watch TV and relax, maybe have a beer or two after work. But my father-in-law had other plans. He liked to play a little game called *Master and Servant.* He would usually show up with his toolbox and then inspect the apartment, looking for things to fix. My role in this drama was the *flashlight man.* I would follow him with the flashlight; just in case we ran into some stubborn darkness. He made it painfully clear during these little exercises that he thought I was useless. I couldn't even operate the flashlight properly. He would always curse, "Damn it, keep the light steady. A little to the left. More to the right. When was the last time you changed the batteries in that flashlight?"

Hanging out with him was like hanging out with a bad rash. He was acutely irritated during these little fix-it sprees because he couldn't understand why I didn't go around fixing stuff on my own.

He had decided I was lazy at some point in our quiet

relationship, or at least he would ask me questions that suggested that he thought I was lazy. He always asked me, whenever he saw me, regardless of the time of day, "Did you just wake up?"

Once he asked me while I shined the flashlight and he screwed a screw, "You're not too good with the tools, eh?" I didn't know if he was referring to screwdrivers and hammers or if he was really referring to the lack of grandchildren. Jenny's mother was always wondering aloud about grandchildren. "When are you going to have some children? That's what this place needs, the patter of little feet." Etc. Whenever she would talk about the absence of grandchildren, which was always, she would give me a concerned, sorrowful look. I never completely understood that look. But it seemed to me that she had concluded I was the kink in her desire to be a grandmother.

*****

One sunny weekend Jenny announced, "Tomorrow, when Mom and Dad come over, I thought we could do a barbecue."

"We don't have a barbecue," I yawned.

"We do now." Jenny took my hand and led me to the balcony. She was thrilled. Standing on our little balcony was a brand new barbecue. It was black and bulbous with skinny silver legs and a curved dish for collecting the ashes. Jenny had even bought me a set of grilling utensils

– spatulas, tongs, a brillo pad on a long stick for cleaning the grill. She gave me a big happy kiss.

"But I've never barbecued anything before."

"My dad will show you how," she said walking away.

Whoa. A grilling lesson from my father-in-law sounded like an awful way to spend Sunday. Men don't go to other men for lessons about grilling meat. Asking for a lesson about sticking meat in a fire was like admitting that you had a foot fetish or that you liked showering with other men. It was unthinkable. Our neanderthal forefathers had invented the barbecue after all. It was supposed to be in my DNA.

The next day her parents came over around 11:30. Jenny announced that we were grilling steaks for lunch. She had bought 4 enormous porterhouse steaks and some corn on the cob. I was outside on the balcony hoping for rain.

"You aren't planning to grill up here are you?" asked my father-in-law. I hadn't given it much thought, to be honest.

"You can't grill on your balcony, you need to take the grill down to the courtyard. If you want, I'll help you," my father-in-law had been prepped by Jenny to offer his help.

"No, don't worry. They used to call me the Grill Master when I was at the university," I lied. This barbecue was bigger than meat, charcoal and flames. This was about manhood: my manhood. Actually, it was about my father-in-laws perception of my manhood.

The elevator was out of service, so I had to carry the grill down the stairs. My father-in-law followed behind me with a six pack of beers. Around the second floor I lost grip of the grill and it crashed down the remaining stairs. My father-in-law seized the moment, "What the hell happened? The thing only weighs 10 pounds?"

I ignored him and put the grill back together. That's when I saw that one of its three legs was badly injured. The grill couldn't even stand straight any more. It leaned severely to one side. I didn't let this phase me though. I got the grill outside and around twelve the grill was ready.

Jenny didn't buy any lighter fluid because she didn't believe in lighter fluid. It made the food taste funny, she had told me. So, I stacked the charcoal on some wadded up balls of newspaper. I put a match to the pyramid of coals and there was fire. There was nothing to it. Kids stuff. Hell, if cavemen could do it, I could do it. I sat at a picnic table near the grill and opened a beer. My father-in-law reluctantly joined me. I drank and tried to enjoy the sunlight.

But I soon learned that keeping the fire lit was trickier than it seemed. After about 10 minutes of irritated silence, my father-in-law grunted, "Hey, Grill Master, the fire's been out for the last five minutes." I looked over at the grill. There was an absence of both flame and smoke. I went over and poked the coals with my tongs. There was nothing happening. The newspaper was ash.

I pretended to study the bag of charcoal. "Yeah, this stuff always gives me problems staying lit. It just needs a little extra fuel." My father-in-law watched me, shaking his head. I wadded up the entire Sunday morning paper. I added more charcoal. This time I added some grass clippings from the lawn for good measure. I scanned the courtyard for other flammable items. One of the ground floor tenants' children had left a Sesame Street doll on their patio. Grover. I thought for a second about putting Grover in the grill. I decided it probably wasn't a good idea. I put a match to it. Flames and smoke. Plumes of smoke. I stood at the grill watching the fire through the smoke, silently hoping that it would stay lit. Soon, though, the flames began to dip, then there were no flames, only some sad puffs of smoke. "You might want to blow on the fire," said my father-in-law. I thought he was still sitting at the picnic table, but he was at my elbow. I took his advice and blew. We both blew. Then he threw in some dried twigs, and slowly the flames returned. Soon everything seemed to be under control.

"Well the coals should be ready soon," I was trying to be optimistic.

"In about a half hour or so."

He was a God damned know it all.

I got another beer. Drinking helped me cope with their visits, but today I felt that I needed extra fuel because I was being heavily scrutinized. I finished my beer in silence. My father-in-law was at the grill with the tongs in his hands. He had usurped my role as *grill master*. I tried not to care, but I couldn't help feeling a little angry. After all, his handy man routine, and now his handling of the grill, were acts of aggression. He had been sending me the message loud and clear: I would always be Mr. Flashlight, following his lead. He was the man of the house. I was the boy. I found the whole dynamic of being a son-in-law depressing. So, I finished my beer and took the three remaining beers back to the apartment. I retired to the living room to watch a little TV.

Two beers later, Jenny came into the living room with a platter of steaks, "Why aren't you outside at the grill?"

"I'm not a griller, Jenny. The whole act of putting meat in fire seems so...so primitive."

Jenny glared at me.

"The whole experience has made me reconsider being a carnivore."

She turned the TV off and pushed the platter of steaks at me.

"Stop being so melodramatic and go grill the steaks."

I sighed, took the platter and marched back to the grill, a prisoner of war.

On seeing me, my father-in-law barked, "Where the

hell have you been, *Grill Master?*"

I said nothing. He handed me the tongs and I pushed the coals this way and that. I could only keep my hands over the coals for about a half of a second before they began to burn. It was a damn hot fire.

"You've got too many coals. The fire's too hot," he told me.

Then I put the steaks on the grill. Flames began to leap from the coals. After a couple of seconds, the flames attacked the steaks like lions ravaging a wildebeest. I pulled a couple of steaks away from the flames. More flames.

"Put the damn lid on the grill," instructed my father-in-law. I put the lid on the grill. Smoke started to billow out the smoke holes on the top of the lid. It was one of those lazy breeze Sunday afternoons, and the whole courtyard was quickly filled with smoke. I was waving the smoke away. My eyes burned and watered. I smelled like I had just escaped from a burning building.

We stood at the grill, not speaking. A squirrel scampered by and raced up a tree. My father-in-law watched the squirrel intently. "Squirrels are pretty interesting," I offered.

"They're God damned rodents. Rats with bushy tails." I was appalled. I had never met someone who didn't like squirrels. They're so cute. I was shocked. How can anyone not like squirrels?

I decided that it was better not to say anything else. After a couple of minutes, I pulled the lid off the grill to see what the hell was happening. Smoke swarmed out of the grill.

"I told you the fire was too hot." It was like hanging out with a bad vibe vortex. He spewed negative energy and blame. "You should have banked the coals, so that the steaks wouldn't be directly over the fire."

I did my best to ignore him and flipped the steaks. All of the steaks had turned greyish, and all the fat around the edges had been burned black. The flames started to leap again. I put the lid back on the grill.

"Do you think you could get me a beer?"

"Don't you think you're drinking too much?" he snapped back.

I assumed it was a rhetorical question and didn't answer. After a while he wandered into the apartment complex. By the time he came back with the beer, I had flipped the steaks and had put the lid back on the grill. He handed me the beer and I drank it in one gulp.

Jenny shouted down from the balcony, "How is everything?" She was pretending to be excited about the barbecue. She was probably hoping that me and my father-in-law were doing some good old fashion grill side bonding. If she only knew.

"Everything's under control," I said.

"The steaks are already burned," added my father-in-law.

Jenny smiled and went back inside the apartment.

"How do you like your steak?" I asked.

"What difference does it make," he shot back.

We stood in silence at the grill. My father-in-law was brooding about something. I could see his jaws clench and unclench. "Don't you think we should check the steaks?" he asked.

It was at this point that I began to feel the weight of the drink. Standing completely motionless was impossible. I was having trouble standing still. Every now and then I would lose my balance and stagger to the right or left.

Being drunk, I also felt chatty, and I had the sudden and rather poignant urge to elaborate my theory on the utility of socks. I am not sure why I wanted to talk about socks, perhaps it was because my father-in-law always wore black socks with his white tennis shoes. I had lost all sense of audience, and so without any forethought I launched into my story.

"One time my dad and me had painted his friend's house. We had painted all day, so this guy's wife made us supper. Really greasy hamburgers with some sort of garlic salad. We ate and then painted a little more.

"Anyway, on the way home my stomach began to act up. It began to gurgle and I had really bad gas. The guy lived out in the boonies. In the middle of nowhere. So, as we were driving I told my dad to stop the car. I raced out and slid down a hill and found myself in a small grove of sycamore trees. I dropped my pants and had this awful diarrhea. The Hershey squirts. You know when you have a bottle of Hershey's syrup and there's not much left in it. You squeeze and squeeze and the bottle spits and wheezes out chocolate syrup. When I was done, I tried to wipe myself with sycamore leaves. It hurt a bit and it was really messy, if you know what I mean. So, I used my underwear. I ditched them there in the grove of trees. No sooner did I have pants buttoned, my stomach began to rumble. I began to worry. What would I do if I had another emergency crap? And that's when I thought, I still have my socks. I was never so happy that I had socks as I was on that day."

My father-in-law looked down at his socked feet. I looked at his socks as well. Then he squinted at me and asked, "What are you trying to say, you want to wipe your ass with my socks?"

"No, of course not," he had missed the point. "I just wanted...I was just trying to say...." I really had no idea what I was trying to say.

He gave me a long benumbing look and added, "I'll go see if Jenny needs any help in the kitchen."

He stomped off to the house. I shifted left then right and thought to myself, *What an asshole.* Once he was gone, I pulled off the lid of the grill. I fought the smoke and saw the steaks. I flipped them. They looked awful:

mostly black with grey brown spots that had not been burned completely. I decided to leave the lid off the grill and let them cook in the open air for a while. I tried to be optimistic, *What the hell,* I thought, *there are some people that liked to eat burned food. Maybe Jenny's mother would like burned steak?*

That's when my neighbor's wife, I couldn't remember her name but her husband was named Roger or Rubin Harper, came meandering into the courtyard. Mrs. Roger or Rubin Harper was dressed in a skimpy yellow sundress and she carried a small plastic bag. She didn't see me as she leisurely wandered about the yard. She found something in the grass, but instead of squatting to pick it up, she bent over and I came face to face with Mrs. Roger or Rubin Harper's black thong.

She stood back up and I looked away. Trying to act nonchalant. I concealed myself a little better behind a bush near the grill and continued to watch, hoping she would find something else to pick up.

I don't know how long I was watching, but as I was standing behind the bush my father-in-law sneaked up on me. "When are you going to bring the God damned steaks in?"

I was startled by his sudden interruption, and before I managed to say anything he was looking in the direction of Mrs. Roger or Rubin Harper. "You forgot about the steaks because you're gawking at your neighbor?"

"I wasn't gawking. I was watching her...I think she's collecting rocks or something."

"Fascinating," hissed my father-in-law.

Mrs. Roger or Rubin Harper bent over. My father-in-law raised his eyebrows, "Watching her collect rocks, huh?" He walked back inside the apartment complex.

I pulled the steaks off the grill and brought them inside. The other food was ready. Baked potatoes were buttered, golden corn on the cob. Jenny and her parents met me at the table. When Jenny saw the steaks, her excitement shriveled and died. "What happened to the steaks?" I explained my theory about burned food to Jenny, "Some people, myself included, like to eat steaks this way. I like my steak a little burned."

Jenny seemed more than a little troubled.

"My father said that you were gawking at Julia."

"Who?"

"Julia, our neighbor."

"Rubin's wife?"

"Richard's wife."

"Richard Harper?"

"Richard Horton and Julia Horton, Jamie. Our next door neighbors."

"You don't even know the names of your own neighbors?" guffawed my father-in-law.

"I was watching her collect rocks, that was all."

The dining room was suffocating with silence.

"Let's eat," I pretended I was excited about the meal.

I got myself another beer. I returned to the dining room and sat down, nearly missing the chair.

"We really don't need to eat the steaks," said Jenny. She seemed to be taking my grilling failure pretty hard. She spoke to no one, she just stared blankly at the potatoes.

"What are you talking about?" I said. "These steaks look great."

I opened the beer and took a sip. Jenny's father had a smug look on his face. He liked to watch me fail, and he especially liked it when Jenny also saw me fail.

"I like my steak a little crunchy," I said and I took the steak on top of the plate.

Jenny took a steak, Jenny's mother investigated the two steaks that were left, trying to find one that was the least burned, but they were both equally charred. She gave up and just took the smallest steak she could find. My father-in-law refused the last steak, "I'll stick to the corn and potatoes."

I cut into my steak. Beneath the burned and charred bits the meat was red and bloody. I cut a piece and popped it into my mouth. It was cold and raw and chewy. It was like eating a bloody rubber band that had been served in an ashtray. I washed down the mouthful with a long drink of beer.

My mother-in-law cut into her steak. "Mine is a bit raw on the inside."

"Do you want me to put it back on the grill?"

She looked terrified.

"We have some leftovers from last night. I'll warm those up," said Jenny.

She dashed off to the kitchen. There was an uncomfortable silence. I chewed my mouthful of steak. Somewhere in the room a fly was buzzing.

My father-in-law, cleared his throat, "So, Grill Master, what's on the menu for next weekend?"

Jenny's mother gasped, "Henry. Stop it."

My mind was a flood land of bad ideas. I took a long drink from my beer and I looked my-father-law in his eyes. I had never really paid much attention to his eyes before and I realized that he had beady black little eyes. "Why don't you bring your dog over next weekend, Henry?"

Jenny's mother gasped. My father-in-law threw his napkin on the table, "DID YOU JUST THREATEN TO GRILL MY DOG?"

Jenny ran back into the dining room for damage control, "What's going on here?"

"Your husband just threatened to barbecue Jonesy," spat my father-in-law.

Jenny looked at me like I was some sort of hideous circus freak or something.

"Listen, I didn't threaten to barbecue anything. I just asked if they would bring the dog over next weekend."

"I asked him what he was going to barbecue and he told me to bring over Jonesy."

Jenny's face was a storm of anger: lightning and brutal rain. She crossed her arms and asked, "Why would you threaten to barbecue my father's dog?"

"The vietnamese eat dog," I had no idea what I was saying. Thankfully, Jenny ignored me. "And why would you tell my father that awful story about wiping yourself with your socks."

I had been betrayed.

"I never wiped myself with my socks," I mumbled.

I felt like I was six years old again and was being scolded by my parents for the time I ran away from home and hid in a church for a couple of hours. Jenny was flanked by her mother and father. A triad of hostile faces.

"So?" asked Jenny.

"OK, it wasn't a good idea I guess. But I swear I was just making a joke. I mean, I could never kill a dog. I wouldn't even barbecue a dog if I found it dead in the street. I wouldn't actually barbecue Bonesy," I was beginning to babble.

My father-in-law stared me down, "You've been married to my daughter for three years, and you don't know the name of our dog?"

"He doesn't even know the names of his own

neighbors," whispered Jenny's mother.

"It's Bonesy," I looked to Jenny for help, but she looked away and shook her head.

"Jonesy," huffed my father-in-law, "The dog's name is Jonesy."

"Jonesy," I repeated dutifully although drunkenly.

And that's when I blacked out.

*****

I'm not sure what happened after that, and I'll never know. The next morning Jenny was sulking in her baggy pajamas. She was sipping coffee, trying hard to pretend that I didn't exist. I was sure that it all had to do with the grilling failure. And that pissed me off. She was always upset when I didn't live up to her expectations. There was no way I was going to apologize for over cooking some steaks and then making a joke about cooking her stepfather's dog. He was asking for it after all, with all his hyper aggressivity.

"So you're not talking to me?"

She said nothing.

"Is this about what I said about Jonesy?"

Not a word.

"Are you upset about the story of me wiping myself with my underwear?" I felt I needed to set the story straight, "I never wiped myself with my socks, Jenny. And I sure as hell didn't want to myself with your step-father's socks."

She looked at me with cold contempt.

"Is this about me looking at Mrs. Horton?"

She got up and put her coffee cup in the kitchen. "Her name is Julia Horton, Jamie. And no, it is not about her," her eyes filled with tears her lips quivered as she spoke, "How could you say those things to my father?"

"About the dog?" I had no idea what she was talking about.

She pushed past me and stamped off to the bedroom.

I had obviously said something else. But I had no idea what.

*****

After the barbecue, my in-laws stopped coming over. The place felt lonely without them. I don't know. I didn't really miss them. Maybe it was my guilt that made me feel that way. Jenny was always preoccupied and unhappy. She flitted around the house like a passive aggressive ghost.

I tried to talk to Jenny about that night a million times, but she wasn't interested. She even told me once, "Why don't you apologize to my father?"

"For what? I honestly don't know what I did." I begged her to tell me. It is difficult being the cause of so much misery, but even worse when you don't even know how you actually managed to cause so much pain. I begged her, "Just tell me what I've done wrong."

OOPS, INC.[2]

This was a big mistake, thought Jamie Dropping as Evan and Ivan scurried around the office opening windows, cleaning up the coffee that had been thrown on the fire, and squawking and swearing in a desperate state of frustrated anger. The Receptionist, who had been alerted of the fire by a string of brutal obscenities from Evan, stood in the doorway, fanning away the smell of the burning paper with her hand. "What

---

2 This was originally published as the third chapter of *The Unsolvable Circus.*

happened in here?" she asked coughing.

Well, what had happened in Evan and Ivan's office was the overly melodramatic resignation of a disgruntled employee named Roy Deedle. Deedle had worked as a technical writer for the past two months, during which time he had come to the conclusion that those two months were the worst of his 36 year life, even worse than the time he had been inadvertently buried alive when he was 5 years old.

After Deedle had barged into the office, he proclaimed, "Working here has been as painful as having the shingles." He then set a document on fire in effigy. The document was supposed to represent Evan and Ivan or maybe it represented the Job. In any case, as the flames began to quickly consume the pages, Roy dropped the flaming document on Evan's desk and said slowly, loudly and emphatically, so no one would miss his meaning, "GO TO HELL."

During this dramatic conflagration of human unhappiness, Jamie sat in a chair near Evan's desk, his mouth hanging open, clutching his briefcase to his chest, telling himself *this was a big mistake.*

*****

The day of Roy Deedle's fiery resignation was also Jamie's first day of work for his new employer, whose ill-advised name was announced proudly on a sign outside the office

Object Oriented Payment Solutions, Inc.

Just prior to the Roy Deedle drama, Jamie had learned from the Receptionist that the woman who had hired him, Ms. Lucy Doff, had been fired a couple of weeks ago. The Receptionist, a rotund woman sipping a Diet Coke and eating potato chips, was well made-up with enormous, fire engine red lips. She seemed ready to betray the most intimate details about Ms. Doff. She began to tell Jamie about Ms. Doff's disastrous accident at the company's Christmas party. "Well, let's just say she and one of Santa's little helpers drank a little too..." Jamie, like a chameleon, changed expressions from nervous amicability to unsettled confusion. He blurted out, "So, who should I talk to if she's been fired?" The Receptionist, clearly insulted that Jamie wasn't interested in Ms. Doff's drunken Yuletide debauchery, said testily, "Well, I guess you'll just need to talk to Evan and Ivan. Won't you?"

With that, she picked up the phone and dialed the internal number for Evan and Ivan's office. "I have a Mr. Dropping here." She listened, nodding in agreement to something she was being told. "OK, OK. But today is Mr. Dropping's *first* day. Ms. Doff hired him." She sang this last part, *Ms. Doff hired him,* with stinging irony. This seemed to be all that needed to be said. With the mention of Ms. Doff, the conversation ended. She hung up the phone and said with a vague smile, "They'll see you immediately."

Just past the Receptionist's desk was the office of the Managing Director, Mr. Bert Trigger. His name was printed in big black block letters across the frosted glass of his office door. Adjacent to his office, was the office occupied by Evan and Ivan. Jamie stopped at their door and knocked. After waiting briefly without a response from the men inside, he opened the door and popped his head inside the office. Jamie was prepared to say, "May I come in," but the words dissolved in his mouth. He was stunned silent by what he saw.

*****

Evan Proxy and Ivan Pattern both looked as if they had just graduated from high school. Jamie saw these "men," with their fresh faces full of youthful blemishes, and thought, they're just kids. After the initial shock, he slowly realized that both Evan and Ivan closely resembled each other. They both wore matching dark business suits, shared the same flat-top hairstyle and, as Jamie was soon to realize, also shared the same voice.

Now, Evan and Ivan, both in their early thirties, considered their youthful appearances a curse. Fellow workers, colleagues and other managers tended not to take them seriously. So, in order to make sure that the employees of OOPS understood they meant business, they were cruel and ruthless bastards. Once upon a time, they had banished an entire department to the storage room as a punishment for disobeying their order of no eating fish in the company kitchen. A tuna fish sandwich was the official cause of the department's exile.

When Evan and Ivan were hired, they were considered maverick geniuses that could streamline the most untamed operations, untangle inefficient processes and, well, help make the bottom line a little more healthy.

Unfortunately, they had not been able to make such a dramatic impact on the culture of OOPS. No one was sure how much longer Evan and Ivan would oversee day to day operations, but most people agreed that "Evan and Ivan put the oops in OOPS" and that "Evan and Ivan put the Inc in Incompetence." For the five years they had been working at OOPS, every day was the same tragedy – budget overruns, missed deadlines, screaming clients, bugs, general mismanaged chaos, aspirin, headaches, panic and fear.

"Mr. Dropping," said Evan from behind his desk, "I am Evan Proxy and this is Ivan Pattern. Please take a seat." Jamie entered the office, closed the door and sat down in a chair near Evan's desk.

"It seems that we have a slight problem here," said Ivan immediately. Their voices were clones of one another. Jamie looked from Evan to Ivan and then back to Evan in disbelief. If you were to close your eyes and simply listen to the two men speak, it would be impossible to tell which of them was actually the source of the words you were hearing.

"What sort of problem?" said Jamie defensively.

"Well, Ms. Doff, the woman that hired you has been..." Evan started to explain.

"I was informed by the receptionist that Ms. Doff was fired. She also explained to me that Ms. Doff took a drunken fancy to a Christmas elf. But, frankly gentlemen, I don't see what this has to do with me." Jamie smiled uneasily. He was not about to let these two high schoolers tell him what to do.

"Well, Mr. Dropping," said Evan slightly irritated by Jamie's abruptness, "Ms. Doff was fired for embezzling money. After she was fired, the Managing Director met with us and we rethought the project that she was supposed to be leading. I believe it was called DEJECTUS? Well, anyway, the Managing Director concluded that the project would be postponed indefinitely."

Jamie could feel his face burning red with embarrassment. He felt as though he was the butt of a malicious practical joke. He began to fidget in his chair, crossing and uncrossing his legs, picking pieces of lint off his pants. "I was hired to work on DEJECTUS," he eventually admitted quietly.

"So you understand our problem," snapped Ivan. "You have been hired by a woman that has been fired, to work on a project that does not exist."

Ivan's statement made Jamie fully appreciate his existential uncertainty. But he refused to accept Evan and Ivan's belief that *he* somehow inherited their problems. Clearly, the problem was theirs. So, he began to prepare a defense and was about to rebut Ivan's statement when Roy Deedle stormed in, and within seconds the office was engulfed with smoke.

As Jamie sat in the cloud of smoke, cradling his briefcase in his arms, wondering what in the world was going on, his wife's ghost suddenly appeared. It wasn't the first time he had seen her ghost, but it was the first time she had appeared outside of his apartment. "I told you not to work for a company called OOPS," she scolded him.

Just as quickly as she had materialized, she vanished.

Jamie began to feel as though he were a fictional character in some sort of unbelievable narrative. He sat motionlessly staring at Evan and Ivan as they raced about. He had a faraway look in his eyes that suggested that no stimuli could possibly reach him. He was staring blanks.

Neither Evan nor Ivan appreciated that Jamie just sat there doing nothing. At one point, Evan yelled at him, "Don't just sit there, do something." With those words, Jamie was yanked from his vacant thoughts and he stood up immediately. But he didn't know what to do, so he simply stood there, cradling his briefcase in his arms. Then Evan exploded, and words vulgar and putrid flew from his mouth like a flock of birds bursting into flight.

The Receptionist appeared in the doorway. "What happened here?" she asked fanning the smoke from her face and coughing.

"Roy Deedle happened here," snarled Ivan waving his arms frantically in order to disperse the smoke.

The receptionist slipped away with a disapproving shake of her head, and within a couple of minutes returned with a blue cloaked cleaning woman. The cleaning woman started to furiously mop up the spilled coffee from the floor, muttering in what was probably Russian, then she cleaned the coffee from Evan's desk.

As the smoke began to clear and the chaos began to settle, Evan told Jamie, "Mr. Dropping, we will have to put this matter to the Managing Director. He should be in the office later today. He will decide your fate." Both Evan and Ivan wore the same smug look on their faces that indicated to Jamie that the door to this conversation was closed. Jamie reasoned that they just wanted to clean up their embarrassment as quickly and quietly as possible.

"Take him down to the technical documentation department," said Evan to the Receptionist. She sighed and rolled her eyes.

"But I'm a software engineer not a technical writer," protested Jamie vainly.

"Stop that! You're only making it worse," Ivan blared at the cleaning woman who was spraying a lemon scented air freshener around the room. The room stank of sweet, smoky lemons.

"Go on, take him," said Evan irritated that neither Jamie nor the Receptionist had budged.

Jamie said nothing else. He no longer had the desire to squabble with Evan and Ivan. These men, like all managers are completely out of touch with reality, Jamie thought. He hoped to have better luck with the Managing Director. Plus, he reasoned, if the Managing Director would decide his "fate" later that day, then what did it matter if he spent the day as a technical writer?

As Jamie turned to leave, Evan called him, "Oh, one more thing Mr. Dropping. Tell Mr. Closing that Roy Deedle has been fired."

What a putz, thought Jamie.

*****

Jamie was escorted to the Technical Documentation Department by the Receptionist. She clearly did not want to take Jamie, and after Jamie had left Evan and Ivan's office she stayed behind to remind Evan and Ivan that it wasn't her job to escort the likes of Jamie Dropping anywhere, especially the Technical Documentation Department. She had infinitely more important things to do. Evan and Ivan pressed her into service, though, because they wanted to make sure Jamie found the Technical Documentation Department and remained there. "The important thing is that he *remain* there," Evan explained. Neither he nor Ivan wanted Jamie to resurface again for the rest of the day. The Receptionist told them that she would escort Mr. Dropping to the basement under protest. They paid her no mind. They simply desired Jamie's immediate absence.

Jamie lagged behind the receptionist as she led him down a narrow spiral staircase to the basement. They descended in what could only be described as hostile amicability. Jamie found the silence a bit uncomfortable, and so he decided that he would make an attempt to repair their damaged relationship. "So, she and the elf had sex?"

"What are you talking about?" The Receptionist was obviously irritated that he had broken the silence.

Jamie thought for a moment about clarifying who and what he was talking about, but he didn't have the courage. He felt that if he were to say much more the Receptionist might viciously beat him.

She led and Jamie followed.

At the bottom of the stairs the Receptionist waited for Jamie. As Jamie exited the steps, he found himself in what appeared to be nothing more than a storage room. Bookshelves, crammed with books and binders, were anchored to the walls of the room. Books spilled off the shelves. Beige file cabinets were stationed randomly throughout the room with no apparent attention to efficient use of space. Atop two of the file cabinets stood broken computer monitors which made the file cabinets resemble some sort of primeval corporate totem poles. There were a couple of large cardboard boxes that were open and overflowing with paper. At the far end of the room was a large table and on the table sat three computers.

As Jamie was taking in this strange officescape in front of him, the Receptionist, clearing her throat loudly, announced, "You have a newcomer."

This sudden and unexpected outburst startled Jamie. He gave the Receptionist a quizzical glance and wondered who she thought she was speaking to. But then Jamie saw them. He hadn't been able to see them since they sat behind the computers at the large table in the center of the room, but people inhabited this land of junk and debris. A man and a woman were now peering at him from over the tops of their monitors. He could clearly make out the tops of their heads and their eyes.

The Receptionist, pushed her way past Jamie and started to climb the stairway. She stopped at the second step and said with a cynical smile, "Welcome to the heart of darkness."

*****

One of the natives of the Technical Documentation Department, that had been sitting behind a computer, ventured out to meet Jamie. His name was Steve, but his colleagues called him Chewbacca because he was gruff, smelled awful and usually moaned loudly about everything and anything.

Steve was a shrub shaped man with a peculiar sense of fashion. His white pressed business shirt was two times too large for him and the shoulders floated around the area of his biceps. He had to wear the shirt sleeves rolled-up simply to expose his hands and eliminate the unsightly clumping of sleeve around his wrists. Steve wore black jeans that were too small, and he was unable to keep them buttoned. His stubborn midsection refused to cooperate. Consequently, his zipper was usually open.

Jamie, who was too shocked by the appearance of the office to move a centimeter from the bottom of the stairs, stood silently watching Steve approach. Steve stopped a couple feet from Jamie, settled into a casually confrontational posture by folding his arms against his chest and leaning back on his heels. He said with a loud and booming voice, "No one told us a new person would start today." Jamie felt awkward as the man examined him with an unfriendly glance.

Jamie explained, "There seems to be a little confusion..." Jamie was prepared to fire off a diatribe against Evan and Ivan implicating them in the most heinous acts of managerial incompetence, when he suddenly realized that this man standing before him was, in fact, bleeding. A trickle of blood ran down his forehead. Jamie shuddered involuntarily at the sight of the blood.

"You're bleeding," he cringed.

Steve pulled a wad of tissue from his pockets and

dabbed his forehead. After each dab he examined the tissue. "My doctor removed a lump from my head this morning." He bowed to show Jamie the wound. The top of Steve's head was shaved and a piece of gauze was taped to his scalp. Jamie peered at Steve's head unwillingly and saw some blood trickle out from the gauze. "He wanted to run a biopsy on it."

Jamie shuddered again and silently wondered if he could somehow get his old job back.

*****

The second native from behind a computer now joined Jamie and the bleeding Steve. She was small, brunette, bright and buoyant. Her face was adorned with a smile which was a relief to Jamie. She was the first person he had met this morning that didn't seem miserable. She smiled and offered her hand, "Hello, I'm Jane." Jamie shook her hand. "Jamie Dropping."

"I see you've met Steve already."

Steve refused to shake hands with Jamie. He stood with his arms folded against his chest, rocking on his heels. "So, what happened to Roy?" he growled.

"Roy's been fired." Without thinking about it, Jamie said these words with great sensitivity, as if he was a close friend of Roy's.

"And you're Roy's replacement?" asked Steve pointedly. "Pretty convenient for you isn't it? Someone gets fired and you get hired." He glared accusingly at Jamie.

"No. I'm a software engineer. I was hired by Ms. Doff..."

"She was fired a couple of weeks ago," chortled Steve. "Embezzling."

"I know..." began Jamie.

"Her boyfriend was a midget," Steve added.

Jamie said nothing.

"He worked as one of Santa's elves at Christmas time."

Again, Jamie said nothing.

"He worked as the Easter Bunny in spring."

"You haven't met Edward yet. He's the manager and wordsmith of the department," said Jane changing the subject. Her smile seemed to be a permanent feature of her face. Even as she spoke, it never slipped from place. As she led Jamie towards Edward's office, she suddenly stopped, made sure that Steve wasn't watching and grabbed Jamie's hand. Jamie was surprised by this gesture. He was not a touchy-feely person and he instinctively felt uncomfortable about being fondled in such a personal way. Then he realized that Jane had placed something in his palm. It was a piece of paper. As secretly as possible, he glanced into the palm of his hand and read the message. It said, *"DOES A TOILET FLUSHING IN THE DARK MAKE A SOUND."*

He felt that the message was a bit odd. He didn't know if he should laugh or provide an answer. Seeing that there was no question mark, Jamie reasoned that maybe it wasn't a question after all. The message had the look and feel of a Zen aphorism. Maybe Jane was an aspiring writer of Zen aphorisms, although obviously talentless. Whether the lights are on or off doesn't affect the sound of a toilet flushing. Maybe, it's a trick question of some sort and I should give it more thought, Jamie eventually concluded, and he slipped the paper into his pocket.

*****

Edward Closing ruled the Technical Documentation Department from a gypsy style construction that was his office. Behind the table where Jane and Steve sat was what appeared to be a partial wall. In reality, it was merely a couple of tall pieces of drywall propped up against file cabinets and cardboard boxes. Behind this drywall facade sat Edward Closing, brooding at his desk.

Edward was 55 years old and had been working for OOPS for the past ten years, the longest of any of the others in the Technical Documentation Department. He was a thin man with a ropy body and a full head of silver hair. He sat at his desk with his shirt sleeves rolled up, his tie slackened, collar unbuttoned, reading a newspaper.

"Edward, we have what appears to be a new person with us," Jane announced.

"Jamie Dropping," said Jamie marching to Edward's desk and holding out his hand.

Edward peered over the top of his bifocals at Jamie and shook his hand, "Nice to meet you." Looking past Jamie to Jane, he added, "But no one told me anything about a new hire?"

Jamie began to explain his presence, "Well, it's a long and complicated story, so let me simplify it a bit. Roy Deedle just lit some sort of document on fire in Evan and Ivan's office and quit. I was hired to start today and to work with Ms. Doff on a project called DEJECTUS. She, as

~110~

you know, was fired, and so Evan and Ivan came up with the truly awful decision to send me, a software engineer, to your department to work for the day until the Managing Director can decide where I belong."

"You don't say," said Edward sourly. He examined Jamie carefully, looking him up and down.

"Well, take a seat Jane. You too James. Did you happen to read this morning's news?"

"No." said Jamie enthusiastically. It was obvious, though, that Edward really wanted to speak to Jane and that he regarded Jamie's presence coldly.

"Well it appears that the Quagmire Incident has taken another strange twist." He pushed the paper towards Jane. Jamie leaned towards Jane and they both read the headline *Dr. Quagmire Recovers Miraculously But Young Angie Vanishes Again.*

"Not again," sighed Jane with a smile.

"Well, that's too bad," said Jamie sitting back in his seat. He, along with all of Ersatz Michigan, had been sucked into the quicksand of the Quagmire Incident at one point or another. But he had grown weary of the story's ins-and-outs, with it's constant airplay and analysis. At this point any news about the Quagmire's was merely anticlimactic. Jamie found the whole thing boring and couldn't understand why people were actually interested any longer.

"The article states that the girl's mother believes that it was the work of aliens. Extra terrestrials. Her daughter was abducted." This last sentence was punctuated by Edward's big, yellow coffee stained smile.

*****

Historically speaking, the Quagmire Incident began the day that the local Ersatz newspaper, the **Eye of Ersatz**, ran the story *Deranged Man Without Pants Attacks Police in Park*. But no one knew that the pantless man was Dr. Harry Quagmire trying to pay off his daughter's kidnappers.

Nonetheless, a day after the pantless Dr. Quagmire had fought with the police, the **Eye of Ersatz** broke the story *Bizarre Kidnapping Leaves One Injured and Another in a Coma*. Apparently, a young girl named Angie Quagmire had been kidnapped and as she was being returned to her father, for the price of $500,000, a shoot-out ensued. Police found a woman, Mrs. Martha Frigs, shot and unconscious in a wooded area not far from the kidnapping. Angie said that Mrs. Martha Frigs had nothing to do with the kidnapping. She had never even seen her before.

But the real news was that Angie's father fell into a coma as he fought with one of the kidnappers. Angie had a theory regarding his sudden coma, but the **Eye** wasn't interested in her outlandish tale.

Strangely enough though, the medical community of Ersatz Michigan concluded that Dr. Quagmire was not comatose. The doctors declared that he was in a "state of suspended animation." When the **Eye** found out that the doctors believed that Dr. Quagmire was in a state of suspended animation, whatever that meant, the reporter rushed back to Angie for an interview. The next day the **Eye** continued the story with the headline *Kidnap Victim's*

Father in a State of Suspended Animation. The story reported that one of the kidnappers was in fact some sort of "witchdoctor." The police made an official statement telling the public that they suspected the use of voodoo and that they were on the lookout for anyone that fit the description of a witchdoctor.

Only a couple of days later, a body was found in the Rex Hotel. A man had been murdered by being drowned in a bathtub full of creamed corn and applesauce. Everyone in Ersatz was shocked about this sudden explosion of violence. Kidnapping and murder didn't happen in Ersatz. At least they usually didn't happen in the same week. So, naturally, everyone in Ersatz started getting nervous, especially the police since they had three kidnappers, one of which was a witchdoctor, and a murderer at large.

Not long after these events, the **Eye of Ersatz** reported some animal bones were found in the yard of Little Lamb kindergarten. An elderly lady, Mrs. Kerwitz, who lived near the kindergarten, said that her dog, a poodle named Frank, had been missing for days. "Frank has never gone missing before," she sobbed to the police.

Animal bones? Missing poodles? Dr. Quagmire's voodoo induced coma like state? The authorities could smell the sulphur burning. They created a list of suspects and atop the list was none other than Satan himself. The police were convinced that Ersatz had dived, head first, into the deepest most rotten pit of hell.

A couple of days later, the suspicions of the Ersatz Police Department were confirmed when a couple of high school students that were searching for a quiet and secluded place to "finish their geometry homework," stumbled into "a drunken satanic orgy." The couple told police that they were "forced to participate in the fornication" and that "blood was everywhere." Naturally, the police assumed that the blood probably belonged to a recently murdered poodle named Frank.

As things began to heat up in Ersatz and as the city buzzed with fear that was as dangerous as a chain-smoking arson working in a gas station, a priest by the name of Father Patrick asked the simple questions, "Are our children safe? Are they out of harm's way?" As it turned out they weren't. Police rounded up the children from Little Lamb kindergarten in order to interrogate them. They suspected that Mr. Harry Wiener, a teacher at the school, worshiped Satan. To the shock of parents, the police investigation found that all the children at the kindergarten had been molested by Mr. Wiener.

The release of this finding sent Ersatz into a Harry-Wiener-hating-destroy-little-lamb hysteria. Naturally, everyone wanted to see Weiner executed. The Little Lamb kindergarten was burned to the ground.

As the smoke and stench of hell began to thicken, the District Attorney of Ersatz County realized, after reading through the transcripts of the interrogated children, that there was no real case against Mr. Wiener. He explained to the police that some of the questions they asked were slightly problematic, in a legal sense, and forced the children to falsely implicate Harry. "Come on guys," he yelled at the chief of police and the detectives in charge of the case. "This will never stand up in court.

Look here, a detective asks a kid, 'Are you sure that Harry Wiener molested you more than once?' The kid responds, 'No.' Then the detective asks, and this is brilliant, 'So you aren't sure he molested you more than once? How many times did he molest you then?' The answer 'Three.' Come on guys!"

So it was that the charges were dropped. The police admitted that they believed Mr. Wiener was, unfortunately, innocent of all child molesting charges, although he was still investigated for links to Satan and the illegal practice of Voodoo. But then Frank the poodle returned home, happily wagging his surgically shortened poodle tail. The case was officially closed.

Ms. Kerwitz, who didn't know where Frank was for all those days, told the **Eye of Ersatz** she was just "glad he was alive and that he hadn't been murdered by a bunch of satan worshiping child molesters like Harry Wiener."

*****

"Extra Terrestrials." Edward seemed ecstatic about the news. He stood up and began to pace about his tiny office.

"The mother stated that she heard a strange noise. She went to her husbands bedroom where she found a strange *grey* man standing over top of him chanting. She said there was a *burst* of *bright light* and she was *frozen*. She couldn't *move*. That is all she remembers. She woke up a couple hours later asleep on the floor. The girl hasn't been seen since."

Jamie and Jane watched Edward as he paced. He walked to and fro mumbling to himself. It was clear that he was wrestling with something big. Suddenly, he stopped and seemed to stare through some invisible window that exposed a glorious new universe.

While Edward stood transfixed, Jane leaned towards Jamie and whispered, "Edward has a web site dedicated to the Quagmire Incident. He's obsessed with it."

"What software systems are you documenting currently?" Jamie whispered back.

Jane was taken aback by the question, her smile twitched nervously and she chuckled. "Roy was the only one who actually worked around here."

Edward stopped pacing. He stood motionless as a revelation came crashing into him with the force of a meteor slamming into a planet. "The Department of Disinformation!" he announced pumping the air with a wizened fist.

*****

Shortly after Edward had launched his site (www.thequagmireincident.com) that presented a "factual day by day analysis of the Quagmire Incident," he was contacted via email by someone that went by the name Ann O'Nymous. It didn't take Edward more than a half hour to realize that Ann O'Nymous was not Irish and that the name was really a playful pseudonym for someone that wanted to remain *anonymous*.

Ann informed Edward that she was a former FBI agent that used to work for the Department of Disinformation. She then began to explain that the information she was providing to Edward was intended for a larger audience. She wanted him to post her information on his website so that the people of Ersatz would "understand what is really going on."

Ann's message to the world was this, "The kidnapping of Angie Quagmire is a fiction. It may have actually happened but it is being constructed and reported in such a way to ensure that other things go by unnoticed. There is a much darker plot at work here. Here are the facts: (1) James Alexander Shade was murdered the night Angie Quagmire was found. (2) James Alexander Shade had written a book titled the *Mass Extinction Event* (I urge all of you to read this book). (3) *The Mass Extinction Event* contains classified information. (4) The FBI sent an agent named Joe Lillywhite to Ersatz Michigan in an attempt to recover classified information that they believed Shade possessed. (5) The FBI Agent, Joe Lillywhite, went missing and has never been found. (6) A second agent, Fred Deller, was sent to find the missing Lillywhite. The day that Deller arrived, the front page news article in the **Eye of Ersatz** was about teenagers stumbling into a drunken satanic orgy (a completely ridiculous and unbelievable story engineered by DoDis in order to thought clog the public in the eventuality that the Lillywhite story would break)..."

There were many, many more facts that Ann reported. In total she listed 258 facts. But she closed with an eerie exhortation, "James Shade's *The Mass Extinction Event* depicts a scenario in which the Government turns war into a reality style TV program. But the program is not for human consumption. The program has been sold to a race of entertainment starved aliens known as QabNoks. These QabNoks are here and working with the Government and Hollywood to create a nuclear war that will be televised throughout the universe. Why? The Universal Governing and Organizing Department (UGOD) thinks that the time for the next mass extinction event on earth is overdue. The residents of this vast universe want to make sure that us *Homo Sapiens* are wiped out before we start exporting our own forms of extinction to other planets." And now the aliens had in fact entered the picture.

*****

"I think it's time to build the ark," said Edward returning to his seat.

"Excuse me?" Jamie had no idea what Edward was talking about.

"The world's coming to an end," Jane whispered smiling.

"If that woman leans over and whispers into your ear one more time, you'll be sorry." Jamie's wife's ghost had appeared again. Her diaphanous face hovered menacingly close to Jamie's. If her nose was real it would have pressed against his. As quickly as she had appeared, she disappeared again.

Jamie had recoiled into his seat. His dead wife's ghost seemed to be getting more and more aggressive. Although she usually never appeared outside of the apartment, she had now made herself visible to Jamie twice at OOPS. He found it very disconcerting.

Now, his dead wife's ghost was not able to do any real harm to anyone or anything. But she could perform annoying pranks, like hide Jamie's car keys.   There was one time where she hid Jamie's keys by burying them in the cat's litter box.

"Will somebody please show me to my desk," he blurted out.

"The world is coming to an end and you want to work?" Edward couldn't believe his ears.   He already disliked Jamie intensely.

"You can take Roy's seat I guess,"   Edward said slowly still trying to comprehend why someone would be interested in work when doomsday was probably only hours away.   Jamie uncoiled himself and stood up with a sigh of relief.   "Maybe you could help Steve with the project he and Roy were working on," Edward said with a frown.

Jamie was preparing to make a quick exit from Edward's shanty of an office when Jane beamed, "I'll show Jamie to Roy's computer."

"No," barked Edward, "you and I have a few things to discuss."

Jamie was relieved that Jane was detained by Edward. His wife's ghost seemed strangely jealous of Jane, and Jamie was acutely frightened of his dead wife's ghost. Jamie scrambled out of the office.

*****

Steve was sitting at his computer picking his nose.

"Where's Roy's computer?" Jamie asked.

"Over there," said Steve. Startled by Jamie's sudden appearance, he quickly and discreetly pulled his finger from his nose and pointed in the direction of Roy's computer. Jamie sat down at the computer and found that it was turned on and that Roy had already logged in.

Jamie took a couple of moments to calm himself and then informed Steve, "Edward said I should take a look at the project you and Roy were working on."

Steve looked up at Jamie and asked squinting, "What?"

Jamie repeated himself a little more loudly, "Edward said I should take a look at the project you and Roy were working on."

Jamie noticed for the first time, that Steve would squint at him whenever he spoke. It was as if he was nearsighted and was trying to read the words as they came out of Jamie's mouth. Accompanying Steve's squint was a grimace of sorts that seemed to suggest that he was suffering some kind of pain, as if Jamie's words poked or painfully prodded him.

"Well you can begin by looking at some files on Roy's computer." Steve joined Jamie at Roy's computer and navigated to the location of the files.

"Now these files," explained Steve using the mouse pointer to indicate the files he was referring to, "document the S.E.A. system. This file contains the source code for the program. It might be of interest to you since you're," Steve paused and gave Jamie a cursory glance and resumed, "a programmer."

"I'm a software engineer," corrected Jamie. "What is the S.E.A. System?"

Again, Steve's face was puckered into a painful squint, "It's the data encryption program used in all data exchanges." Steve returned his attention to the files, "This file documents the algorithm used by S.E.A. It's a good starting point," he said as he opened the file. Once the file opened, Steve stared at the computer monitor in disbelief. He closed the file and opened it again. "Hmmm," he said. It struck Steve strange that the file was empty of all content except for one word. And this word stood like a monument in the center of the page.

PUD

"Hmmm," Steve repeated himself. He opened another file, then another file. Eventually, he opened all the files, and they all contained the same single word.

"You must have a virus," concluded Steve.

Jamie knew this was no virus. This was a premeditated act of vandalism.

"This is not good," grunted Steve.

"Don't you have any backups?" asked Jamie hopelessly.

Steve shook his head, "No. But we do have hard copies of these files..."

Steve went to a bookshelf and jerked out a white binder that was firmly wedged between other white binders. Licking his index finger and his thumb, he began to page through the binder. As he turned the pages, it became clear to Jamie that what Steve was looking for was missing. Steve would stop and backtrack. He had a puzzled look on his face. Steve went back to the bookshelf and he stared at the countless white binders. A trickle of blood ran down his forehead.

*****

Steve searched through numerous white binders. The back of his shirt, around his collar, was wet with sweat, and pools of sweat had collected at his armpits. He stood hunched over the latest binder he had taken from the bookshelf, dabbing his forehead with his wad of tissues.

"Aha," said Steve suddenly. "I've found something." He put the binder in front of Jamie who had been concentrating desperately not to think about anything that his wife's ghost might find offensive. He was afraid that his dead wife would make an unwanted appearance again. His right hand was buried in his pants pocket firmly clutching his car keys.

"This is the source code for the S.E.A. system," said Steve with a sweaty smile.

Jamie said nothing as he returned from the faraway land of his psychic turmoil. "It's written in a language called Cod," Steve explained.

"Cod? I've never heard of it," said Jamie. He looked at the page of code and nearly wept. The first line read,

a(em%12;-fuDx2mch;9yt$(b[em
%poo;vary;x]))=fred.

"Are you serious?"

"Oh yeah, that's Cod," said Steve.

Steve flipped past the pages of source code and he stopped at another page of plain text and said, "And this is an example of the encrypted text. Roy called it 'poop-text.'"

As Jamie read the text he understood why Roy had called it *poop-text*. It was a rather long story containing incoherent and freakish characters, and filled with references to the scatological. Poop and toilets abounded.

"Are you sure this is the encrypted text?"

"Yeah," Steve said simply. "S.E.A. Scatological Encryption Algorithm," he added with a shrug as if it were obvious.

"Scatological Encryption Algorithm?" choked Jamie. He couldn't believe what he was being told. "This is not the encrypted text," he insisted. "This is probably what was used *for* encryption. It's some sort of silly joke."

Jamie tried to hand the page back to Steve, but Steve was not in the mood to take it. He was irritated by Jamie's disbelief. He stood motionlessly. Jamie shook the paper impatiently at Steve and said, "Here, take it."

"It *is* the encrypted text," protested Steve. "Hold the paper to the light."

"Hold it to the light?" The idea was preposterous.

"Hold it to the light," moaned Steve loudly.

Jamie sighed and held the paper to the light. Steve looked at the paper eagerly. "Do you see it?" Jamie was irritated beyond words.

"See what?" he asked dully.

"The original text."

Jamie looked at the paper and was astounded. He could clearly see words contained in the words of the poop-text. Floating about in the shadows of the poop-text was a subtext, the original text.

Jamie took a moment to think and said, "Wait a second. The whole point of encryption is to disguise a message, making it unreadable through the application of some sort of algorithm. Here the text of the message is encrypted but the original text is also contained in the encrypted message?"

What Jamie had just said didn't make much sense to Steve, or to Jamie for that matter. Steve shrugged his shoulders and then pulled the page from Jamie's hands. "You're the programmer not me."

*****

Jamie had made a concerted effort to understand

Cod syntax. But after 3 minutes he quickly realized this endeavor was a colossal waste of time. He asked Steve, "Do you have a programmer's manual for Cod?"

"No," said Steve bluntly.

Jamie thought for a moment and then asked, "Do you have a Cod compiler? Maybe I could understand something if I could walk through the Cod."

"I just document the stuff. I don't write Cod. You probably need to ask somebody upstairs about a compiler."

What's the use, thought Jamie. Roy had erased an area of arcane knowledge so effectively that the effort of trying to restore it seemed ridiculous. Jamie had nowhere to start. Even if he were able to track down a Cod compiler he knew that he would have to be nothing less than a psychic to actually understand the syntax of the language. It was impossible.

Out of curiosity, Jamie decided to see what he could find on the Internet. Maybe, just maybe, he could find some resources for Cod developers? He searched for "Scatological Encryption Algorithm Cod".

Unfortunately, the Internet provided no help. Jamie's search produced a single website. It was a forum for struggling writers who had suffered countless rejections. The name of the site was "Struggle & Rejection." One member, Frankfa, had posted a message

```
Does anyone think that the following would
make for a good story?  It is set in the
distant future where the greatest killer of
earthlings is spontaneous combustion.  Well, a
```

man working for the **Scatological** Institute of America (SIA not to be confused with the CIA haha :o)) who spends his working days examining the fecal matter of ordinary Americans in order to make sure that no one is rebelling from the strict diet imposed by the diet police (a group of fascists that like to beat people up if they find them eating things like sardines and pineapples), has reoccurring dreams about a talking fish, maybe a **cod** or a trout, that keeps telling him 'Spontaneous combustion is 96% more likely in people that own poodles.' So he proclaims that he knows how to save people from combustion. People need give up their poodles. This is difficult since poodles are owned by almost everyone because their fur is used to make clothing. So, people start giving up their poodles and combustion seems to slow down. Soon everyone is giving up their poodles and the man is a hero. But then one day, a non-poodle owner combusts. More and more non-poodle owners start to combust. As it turns out people get fed up with him and an angry mob kills him. As he dies he sees the fish again and this time it tells him, "It was doodle not poodle, you asshole....Spontaneous combustion is 96% more likely in people that don't doodle.

The only response was from, Little Wille ShakeYerSpear, "Frankfa, that would be interesting. Maybe you could make the fish a parrot though, since a talking parrot is more believable than a fish. Just an idea."

Jamie silently pondered the plot of Frankfa's story and tried hard to imagine a future in which everyone was wearing clothing made of poodle fur. Suddenly, the new mail icon appeared at the bottom of Roy's screen. Roy had mail and Jamie felt curious. He cautiously and furtively opened the email program. He opened Roy's Inbox just as Jane came out from behind the wall that shielded Edward from the other workers. She announced with a smile, "Edward has called for a meeting."

*****

The meeting was held in Edward's office. Jane sat in a chair close to Edward's desk. Jamie took the chair opposite Jane, and Steve sat behind them. Edward handed a sheet of paper to Steve and Jamie as they sat down.

"Listen, this is a new ending. I am not at all satisfied with it, though. It still needs a lot of work, and now that new information has come to light regarding the end of life on Earth, I think that it is a rather futile task trying to finish this novel."

Jamie began to read. The title at the top of the page read "Someone is Sleeping with My Dead Wife." He gasped aloud as he read the words *Dead Wife.* Just the reference to a dead wife gave him the jitters. As he continued to read, the words were lost as his thoughts continually seemed to fall into orbit around the idea of his wife's ghost.

"I think it's great," boomed Steve. "This is *the*

ending. I mean this is really, really great."

"No, I'm not so sure..." said Edward blushing a little.

"And it ends with the sentence, 'Mr. Humpy flushed the toilet.' That's poetry."

"Thanks Steve, but I think you are being a little hasty. Take some time and read it more carefully," Edward said uncomfortably pulling at his collar.

"What do you think Jamie? You probably find it a bit offensive? Or maybe you find it misogynistic?" Edward tried hard to fish out some cutting criticism from the newcomer.

Not one of the words that Jamie had read had actually reached him. He sat there with the page in his hands consumed by thoughts of his wife's ghost. "Well..." he began but he stopped there.

"*TO READ AN ENDING WITHOUT READING THE REST OF THE STORY IS LIKE POOPING AND FINDING THERE IS NO TOILET PAPER*," said Jane aphoristically. She winked at Jamie.

Edward pulled at his nose. He huffed and he hawed. He knew that Jane was right. Jamie couldn't possibly understand the ending without knowing a little about the story. So Edward summarized, "The title of my novel is *Someone is Sleeping with my Dead Wife*. It's about an old man named Mr. Humpy. He's an extremely wealthy octogenarian whose trophy wife dies from breast cancer. Shortly after her death he has her cryoperserved. At first the novel leads us to believe that this cryopreservation is an act of love – a husband's attempt to give his wife life again. But by the end, we realize that Mr. Humpy is not motivated by love. Rather, he is acting out of fear. He fears the loneliness that he was trying to escape by marrying such a young woman in the first place. He fears life without the woman that he believed would long outlive him. Shortly after her cryopreservation, he begins to have terrible and troubling fantasies about his dead wife being violated sexually by the staff at the Cryonic Center where she is preserved in cryostasis. This, of course, is a clear and obvious metaphor that Mr. Humpy is beginning to realize that he truly has lost his wife. And how does he respond to this loss? He gets angry and decides to have her cremated. So, in the final pages of the story we witness the base hatefulness of which Mr. Humpy is capable. The page that you are holding in your hands is that page. Mr. Humpy takes the ashes of his dead wife to his home, proceeds straight to the bathroom, opens the lid, and then dumps her remains. He closes the lid. The story ends with Mr. Humpy flushing the toilet."

*****

"This is a fine mess you've gotten yourself into," scolded Jamie's wife's ghost. "Why don't you tell them how *I* died?"

The color drained from Jamie's face. He felt as though the air was getting thin and he had trouble breathing.

"Go on, tell them. Tell them about how I *fell* off the balcony of our apartment." Jamie and his wife had once lived happily on the 5th floor of an apartment building. But at some point, Jamie wasn't sure when, things started going wrong. Desperately wrong.

"Listen, don't feel ashamed to tell me that you don't like the ending. I feel that there is something missing. Something isn't quite right," prodded Edward.

"Edward, I don't think you want to finish your story. I think you suffer from the classic male pattern of failure: performance anxiety. You will never succeed because you are afraid of success," Jane's static smile shined as she berated Edward.

"Tell them about me. Tell them about us," the ghost of Jamie's wife gloated.

"Franz Kafka never finished any of his novels. *The Castle* ended in mid sentence..." protested Edward more than a little irritated that Jane was attacking his virility.

"*FEAR IS LIKE A TOILET FLUSHING. IT MAKES A LOT OF NOISE AS IT REPLENISHES ITSELF,*" Jane adopted the air of a Buddhist dispensing wisdom. "Finishing your novel means that you need to give it to other people to read and you are afraid that people may not like it. So, you sabotage your novel to avoid potentially harsh criticism."

"You want an ending?" shouted Edward turning red with anger. "Here is your ending." He wadded the page into a ball and threw it at Jane. It hit her in the forehead and then fell to the ground.

Jane turned to Jamie and said through her permanent smile, "Do you think you could save me from all the mistakes I have ever made?"

"Save *her*? What about me Jamie? You didn't save me, now did you?" echoed the ghost.

This was all too much for Jamie. He couldn't take

any more. He jumped to his feet and he howled, "It wasn't my fault. You committed suicide. You killed yourself."

Silence descended on the room like a vulture descending on a bloody carcass.

"You pushed me. All those years I wasted with you. It was one big push," Jamie's wife's ghost accused bitterly. With that the ghost vanished and Jamie collapsed into his chair nearly in tears, utterly defeated.

"I think I'll go speak with the managing director now," Jamie whimpered lifelessly.   But he didn't move from the chair.

"Or maybe a psychiatrist," quipped Steve quietly.

*****

After a couple moments of respite, during which all was calm, Edward said tenderly, with an almost apologetic tone of voice,   "Jamie, I think that there is something you should know. There is no managing director...he is a fiction...a creation of Evan and Ivan in order to stabilize this environment...in order to give it meaning." He knew that this information would be unsettling, but he believed Jamie needed to know the truth.

Jamie, though, did not appreciate the *truth* as Edward envisioned it.   Instead it triggered an explosion inside him.

"There's no Managing Director?   He's a fiction?" Then Jamie turned on him and said with acidic sarcasm, "Another theory from Edward Closing.   The man that believes the Earth is going to be plunged into a state of war in order to entertain some aliens. Well, you can take your stupid theories and shove them up your ass." Jamie stormed out of the room.

He grabbed his briefcase from Roy's desk. As he grabbed the briefcase something caught his attention on the computer screen. At the top of messages in the Inbox queue was an email from none other than Bert Trigger. The subject of the message, "Your services have been terminated." Jamie chuckled malevolently.

As he opened the email he said loudly, hoping that the others in Edward's office would overhear him, "There's no Managing Director huh? Well look who just sent Roy a message."

The message read:

Dear Mr. Deedle,

This is just a simple note reminding you that you have in fact been fired from the organization. Effective immediately. If you are reading this email you must be still in the building. Please leave.

Best of luck in your future endeavors.
Bert Trigger
Managing Director
OOPS, Inc.

What a dope, thought Jamie as he printed the message. He couldn't believe the stupidity of the email. This Bert Trigger must be made of the same managerial material as Evan and Ivan. But Jamie also felt wonderful. This message was the one single blow that would destroy Edward's house of sticks. The Managing Director existed. He wasn't "a fiction." He was sitting in his office sending pathetic emails to Roy Deedle. He pulled the page off the printer and strutted back into Edward's office.

He walked with a victorious stride past Steve and Jane. He stopped at Edward's desk. He then slammed the email down on Edward's desk. "No managing director, eh Ed?"

"What the hell is this..." Edward started to read the email. Once he finished, he looked up at Jamie, shaking his head as if to say, "You'll never get it, will you?"

Edward reclined in his chair, placed his hands behind his head and said, "We all receive emails from Mr. Bert Trigger. But emails only prove virtual presence, and virtual presence is very different from actual existence." Edward then sat upright and spat, "So, if you don't mind, why don't you take your damn email and shove it up *your* ass."

Jamie was confounded. Befuddled. Never in his life had he experienced such profound skepticism. He didn't know what to say or how to respond to the ridiculous argument that an email from the managing director did not entail that the managing director actually existed. He had the sudden desire to light something on fire, or to break something. But, being that he was brought up to respect the property of others, even if they were mentally deficient, he simply echoed the words of Roy Deedle from earlier that day, "GO TO HELL," he said viciously. He snatched the email from Edward's desk and he turned and fled from Edward's office.

Jamie ascended the spiral staircase without looking back. He exited the underworld of Edward Closing and left the Technical Documentation Department embroiled in a debate over a novel that ended with a toilet flushing.

*****

As Jamie entered the upstairs office he saw that the lights had all been turned off and that everyone was gone for the day. He checked his watch and was amazed to see that it was already 5:55. He quietly strolled over to the receptionist's desk and saw that there seemed to be signs of life in Bert Trigger's office. The lights were on and he heard a voice coming from inside the office. Jamie wished he had dragged Edward up the stairs with him so that Edward could see the managing director with his own eyes. Jamie knocked at Bert Trigger's office door. The voice suddenly stopped speaking. He listened closely at the door. He knocked again, this time with a little more bravado. The door swung open and Jamie stood face to face with Evan and Ivan.

"Can we help you Mr. Dropping?" asked Evan.

"No. I am here to see the Managing Director, Mr. Bert Trigger," said Jamie angrily.

"Well, he didn't make it in today, unfortunately. He should be here tomorrow," said Ivan.

"Oh really?" said Jamie loudly. "That's strange because I have an email here from Mr. Bert Trigger." Jamie held up the printout of the email so that Evan and Ivan could read it. "If Mr. Trigger wasn't here today, then who sent this email?"

Evan stared hatefully at Jamie while Ivan read the email from over Evan's shoulder.

"Wait a second. This email is addressed to Roy

Deedle not to you. Reading another employee's email, even if they happen to be fired, is not allowed. This is grounds for termination," barked Ivan.

Jamie thought that Evan and Ivan were a couple of morons. He knew, not with absolute certainty but with a degree of probability which he believed gave him the right to call it *knowledge*, Evan and Ivan were behind the email to Deedle. He didn't know what kind of game was being played at OOPS, Inc. but something very strange was going on. The idiotic email had to be from the likes of them.

"You're fired, Mr. Dropping," said Evan with a deadpan expression.

"Oh, no," guffawed Jamie. "The only schmuck that is going to fire me is the Managing Director. So, if he happens to arrive tomorrow, he can fire me if he wants. If he doesn't come tomorrow then I'll wait until he does come."

Jamie turned on his heels and walked away. He felt victorious. He felt like a conqueror. He had shown those two cow headed middle-managers a thing or two. Fire me? But Jamie neglected to think about what he had just won, if you could even call it winning. He was still employed for a company called OOPS and he would have to face Evan and Ivan in the morning. Maybe he would even have to face Edward, the thought of which made Jamie boil with anger because he knew that Edward would twist the absence of the Managing Director into support for his theory that no Managing Director existed.

As Jamie exited the building and walked to his car in the parking lot, he thought about the matter carefully and concluded that he could easily counter Edward's ridiculous arguments with the counter-argument that an email from the Managing Director did not mean that the Managing Director had to be in the office to send it. He could have sent it from home? In light of such reasoning, Jamie even began to think that his argument with Evan and Ivan was a bit rash. Maybe they were telling the truth? Maybe, just maybe, the Managing Director did send the email? Impossible. Evan and Ivan had to have written the email.

There were only a couple cars still parked in the parking lot. Jamie reached into his right front pants pocket for his keys, but they were gone. He tried his other pockets. No Keys. He searched his coat pockets knowing, though, that the search was futile. He knew exactly what had happened to his keys. His dead wife's ghost had taken them. He couldn't stand the torment any longer. He suddenly burst into a fiery rage. He began to beat his car with his briefcase. It is hard to say what the act of attacking his own car represented to Jamie, perhaps the car represented Evan and Ivan, perhaps OOPS, or maybe his dead wife, or maybe himself. Nevertheless, he beat the windows, the doors, the hood. He banged and dented the car with a psychotic fury. He then jumped onto the hood of the car, he was determined to break the windshield. He raised his briefcase high over his head and brought it down with a thud. The briefcase popped open and Jamie's papers fluttered out.

A light breeze scattered the papers about the parking lot. Jamie looked up and saw two faces peering at him from an office window. Evan and Ivan. He threw the briefcase at the window. It fell short and landed in a small patch of grass near the front entrance of the building. He gave them the finger and began to dance on the hood of his car.

Evan and Ivan stood at the window of Bert Trigger's office watching Jamie's act of needless violence. Their day had begun with a fire and was now ending with this bizarre display of a man destroying a car with his briefcase. "It's just one of those days," sighed Ivan.

*****

Jamie's wife's ghost had surreptitiously managed to wrangle the keys from her husband's right front pants pocket during his heated exchange with Evan and Ivan. She was able, by ghostly means of inter dimensional transport, to take those same keys into the bathroom. She looked around for a good place to hide them. Where could she hide them? In the garbage? Under the sink? The sinister idea came to her in a flash. Her ghostly and transparent face lit up with otherworldly happiness as she flushed them down the toilet.

Bloody Boots Buried in The Sand

It is Wednesday, 5:30 in the afternoon and not a soul has stepped foot into the Old Strandedburg, the restaurant where 19 year old Jamie Dropping works as a waiter.

It is a typical Wednesday afternoon. The cook and dishwasher occupy the kitchen. The cook swats at flies and reads the sports section of yesterday's newspaper. The dishwasher is picking dirt from underneath his fingernails with a fork listening to the oldies on the radio. The song playing: *See You In September* by the Happenings.

Jamie Dropping is seated at the bar reading Professor Thurme Swinecraft's *The Embedded Persona*.

Professor Swinecraft, a controversial philosopher

and literary critic, had developed the astonishing theory of *the embedded persona* one day while he was mowing the lawn. As he pushed and pulled the mower around some hedges and bushes, and as his genius philosophically contemplated whether the bushes were real or a figment of his imagination, he was struck by a revelation: *All of reality is text. We are embedded within it.* Thus was born one of the most controversial theories in the history of philosophy.

According to the theory of the Embedded Persona, readers should embed themselves into the books they read. They should not be passive participants of the text, but they should *celebrate* the text by making themselves a part of it. In his seminal work, *The Luke Experiment*, Professor Swinecraft put his theory into practice. He embedded himself into the Gospel of Luke as Christ's thirteenth apostle, a jew of "Gaulish origin", named Pierre.

One day Jesus called the one named Pierre to follow him. He was a seller of footwear especially favored by Roman soldiers. Pierre left his footwear stall in the market and followed Jesus. He gave a party much like the one that Mathew gave Jesus, because Mathew was a braggart and had said that none of the other disciples could ever throw such a wonderful party. Jesus, of course, was the guest of honor.

Pierre had organized a splendid buffet, and for entertainment he had rented gladiators from his Roman friends. To the amazement of the crowd, the gladiators juggled midgets and other small objects. The disciple named Simon, who Jesus would later name Peter, was not happy about the party. "Master, how can you stand this party? This place is filled with Romans?" Mathew who was a bit jealous about being outdone by Pierre even added, "I don't think he is a good choice. Even the Pharisees seem to like him." But Jesus heard none of this. He rebuked them both and told them, "Pierre will be the feet that will deliver my message."

(*The Luke Experiment, p.122*)

And of course, *The Luke Experiment* ended with perhaps the most astonishing claims in the history of modern philosophy. Professor Swinecraft had argued rather eloquently that this experiment was not some sort of "literary vandalism" as his lifelong antagonist Dr. Clive Polygoat had claimed, but it had convinced him of the truth of Christ's resurrection. Professor Swinecraft had stated, "With the Luke Experiment, I witnessed the resurrection of Christ. Pierre saw it with his own eyes, thus I saw it with my own eyes."

The embedded persona claimed that by writing yourself into a text you are able to experience what the characters actually experience. The theory promised that if you were reading a book and you wanted to know what someone looked like, if you wanted to solve a mystery or if you wanted to know what was true and what was false, you just needed to write yourself into the book and discover the answers for yourself.

Dr. Clive Polygoat considered the theory phenomenally problematic, but most of his criticisms were simply grotesque *ad hominem*s. He had proclaimed after reading the *The Luke Experiment,* "Any muddleheaded moron can write himself into the Bible and claim whatever lunacy he wants but it doesn't make it true. I can write myself into the book of Jonah as another whale and swallow Jonah after the other whale spits him out. Professor Swinecraft would like us to believe that I actually know what Jonah tastes like?!? Utter nonsense. Professor Swinecraft's *Luke Experiment* did convince me of something: he is a complete ass."

Little does Jamie Dropping know, but in ten paragraphs time, a customer will arrive. The only customer of the day. Will he be a big tipper? No, but he will be wearing a short sleeved suit coat.

*****

The door opened and in bounded an old man. The man wore a short sleeved suit coat – beige with a stain just above the right pocket. But even more striking than his strange sense of fashion were his testicles, which were enormous. It looked as if the old man had a cantaloupe stuffed down the front of his pants. Because of the size of his balls, he didn't walk or shuffle but he bounded from leg to leg, slowly bouncing his way into the Old Strandedburg restaurant.

Jamie put down his book and walked over to the table where the man sat and poured him a glass of water.

The old man took a tentative sip. "The water tastes a little funny."

"We put fresh mint in the water."

"Hmmm. No, it's not mint. It's more like the molecular decay of plastic. That pitcher is most likely

~142~

very old and the plastic molecules have probably come loose and are mixing with the water. I have very sensitive taste buds."

"Are you sure it's not the mint?"

"Positive."

Jamie handed the old man a menu. The man took two napkins and used them to avoid touching it with his bare hands. The man could sense Jamie's speculation. "I don't like touching things that have been soiled by a myriad of others." He studied the menu briefly. "I'll take the cheeseburger, but hold the cheese."

"I'm sorry, sir, you said a cheeseburger with no cheese?"

"That is correct young man."

"So, you want a hamburger."

"No, I want a cheeseburger with no cheese. It is a little known fact, but cheeseburgers are both tastier and more tender then hamburgers."

"We can cook the hamburger medium rare..."

"Oh no, please, no blood."

"Cheeseburger no cheese. Would you like anything to drink?"

"Just water, but from a glass pitcher that has been manufactured in this decade, please."

Jamie took the menu, and the old man also gave him the napkins he had used to handle the menu.

In the kitchen, Jamie announced to the cook. "We've got this real pain in the ass customer. He wants a cheeseburger with no cheese."

"So, the asshole wants a hamburger," yawned the

cook.

"No he wants a cheeseburger with no cheese. He says he can also taste plastic molecules in the water."

"What?"

"Yeah, well we'll give that bastard a cheeseburger with no cheese," muttered the dishwasher.

"Have you guys ever seen a short sleeved suit coat before?"

No one responded.

Jamie went back to his book.

*****

It is at this point in our story that Jamie Dropping encountered two terms that Professor Swinecraft had invented to help explain his theory: the fictive-real and the real-fictive. A great deal of confusion still surrounds these terms even to this day because these terms are mirror images of each other. They are like identical twins – impossible to discern the one from the other. There are those that have dedicated their academic careers to the theory of the embedded persona and they still wonder at times, "Am I thinking about the real-fictive or the fictive-real?"

Professor Swinecraft had explained these terms thusly:

The real-fictive is the text and the fictive-real is the text about the text. These terms are the heartbeat of the theory of the embedded persona. Without them the theory would not be able to live. Indeed it is the meeting of these two terms that probably caused the initial explosion of the universe. You and I, all of creation, participate in the grand celebration of text. We are embedded personas in the real-fictive which is expressed in the fictive-real.

(*The Embedded Persona, p.12*)

Jamie flips this paragraph over in his mind the same way that the cook flips the hamburger. He turns it this way and he and he turns it that way. But he can't cook the concept. Even as the flames leap from his mind, the fictive-real and the real-fictive remain raw.

He stops and begins to skim through the rest of *The Embeded Persona*. It is a thick book, slightly thicker than a standard dictionary, and he has a long way to go. His heart sinks. He turns to the last page. There is a picture of Thurme Swinecraft at the age of 38. The Professor looks particularly dapper. Jamie takes a closer look at the photo, and he sees something strange. He then looks at the old man who has just ordered a cheeseburger without cheese. They resemble each other greatly. They are both wearing a short sleeved suit coat.

*****

Ding. The cook rang a bell and pushed a plate with a hamburger onto the counter.

Jamie walked to the the kitchen, but he didn't take his eyes off the old man. It was him. He was certain of it. He then rushed the burger to him.

"Here you are sir, your cheeseburger with no cheese."

The man pushed the bun off the burger and examined the meat patty by putting his face close to the burger and taking a deep breath.

"Sir, I know this may sound strange, but I was

wondering if you are in fact Professor Thurme Swinecraft?"

The man glared at him. "Have you been sent by Dr. Polygoat?"

Jamie took this as a yes. "No. I just happen to be studying your theory of the Embedded Persona for my literary criticism class. I was actually thinking of using the theory to interpret the Gerald Monkley's novel *Bloody Boots Buried in the Sand*."

"Bloody Boots Buried where?" Professor Swinecraft found the title appalling.

"*Bloody Boots Buried in the Sand*. Are you familiar with it?"

*****

Cowboy Slim Whitback moseyed into Harvey Dickslop's Saloon. The place was dark and filled with flies. It stank terribly of horseshit. The drunken cowhands of Harvey Dickslop were lurking in the shadows, drinking heavily. The sun stood somewhere between 10 o'clock and high noon. Slim spit on the dirt floor, removed his hat and wiped the sweat from his forehead leaving behind a streak of brown dirt.

"I'm looking for a man named Harvey Dickslop."

"What makes you think that yer gonna find Harvey Disckslop in this here Saloon?" asked the bartender cleaning a whiskey glass with his apron.

"The sign says this place belongs to Harvey Dickslop."

"Well, this place happens to be named Harvey Dickslop's Saloon, but that's jus a name. Before this place

was called Harvey Dickslop's saloon it was called Peggy's Cathouse. Now, would you go lookin in a place called Peggy's Cathouse for some guy named Harvey Dickslop."

Slim sucked his teeth and tried to unravel the riddle of the bartender, but Slim Whitback wasn't born to philosophize about the names of places. No, he was born and raised to move cattle and shoot people who deserved to be shot. "I probably wouldn't mister."

Someone belched horribly.

"So then, why would you figger that a man named Harvey Discklop is here? Just because his name is hoisted above the front door?"

Slim scratched his head. "So, I guess he ain't here, then." No one answered. He could feel the lear of the cowhands that were still sober enough to lear and he added, "If you do see this Harvey Dickslop, then you tell him that Slim Whitback wants a word with him."

(Bloody Boots Buried in the Sand, p. 140)

****

"It's a story about this cowboy named Slim Whitback who is tracking down a missing woman of ill repute named Aphrodite Blosom. Slim fell in love with Aphrodite at first sight. Anyway, I was thinking of embedding myself in the story as Slim Whitback's Native American sidekick, Slowpoke Joe. Pretty good name, huh? Slim finds Aphrodite's bloody boots, but he never finds her. I am convinced that the bartender is actually Harvey Dickslop and of course Harvey Dickslop had something to do with Aphrodite's disappearance."

The idea of using the theory of the embedded

persona on a silly book about cowboys and cowgirls didn't sit well with Professor Swinecraft.   His theory was developed with works of literature in mind: *The Grapes of Wrath*, *To Kill A Mockingbird*, *As I Lay Dying*, *The Great Gatsby*, *Moby Dick*...

"Hmm. Sounds like a truly dreadful book."

"It's sold ten million copies world wide. It's been translated into over 37 languages."

"Book sales and literature, have a negative correlational value. You are aware of that, aren't you? The more a book sells the more likely it is an artifact produced for mass consumption. Literature, my young friend, is something altogether different. Did you know that Mr. William Faulkner sold 200 copies of *The Sound and the Fury* during his life? Of course, Mr. William Faulkner went on to win the Nobel Prize for Literature. I doubt that Gerald Monkley will share the same fate."

"But you've never read *Bloody Boots Buried in the Sand*."

*****

Slowpoke Joe arrived to help Slim Whitback find Aphrodite Blosom. He rode into Slim's camp near a river.

"Hello, Slowpoke Joe."

"How, Slim."

"Whacha doin out this way?"

"I come to help you find missing white woman."

The mere allusion to Aphrodite Blosom sent Slim into a revelry. "Aphrodite was a woman of fine upbringing. She had some of the most well formed legs a man has ever seen. Her toes were perfectly even. All the same length,

~148~

or at least it seemed that way."

Slowpoke Joe kept quiet.

Slim continued, "She had strong legs too. But her feet were so purty. So dainty..."

Slowpoke Joe changed the subject, "We talk to bartender when sun rises."

"I already talked to the bartender and he's a purty smart fella. He's so smart I couldn't understand a damn word he said."

"He Harvey Discklop. He know where woman is."

"How do you know that Joe?"

"I have dream. Bloody Boots in sand. Apron flapping in wind. White woman screaming."

"Well, I'll be."

(Jamie Dropping embeds himself as Slowpoke Joe (Bloody Boots Buried in the Sand, p.145))

*****

"Would you mind if I asked you a few questions, professor? I am having some trouble with the real-fictive and the fictive-real..."

"Let me warn you, this theory is not for the mentally incontinent. It is not an easy theory to grasp. You must be tenacious."

"I think that I am up for the challenge. But tell me, the real-fictive you define as the 'the text.' The fictive-real is 'text about the text.' But you also say that the world is text. So, what I understand is this: the world and all of our experiences of the world is the real-fictive. All text about the world: newspapers, movies, books, news reports, even what I am saying right now are the fictive-real?"

"Ah, you have made a classic mistake. The same mistake that Clive Polygoat made all those damned years ago. Polygoat was weak minded. He had an innate stupidity that blurred his vision of the theory. My young man, the fictive-real and the real-fictive are the yin and the yang. They are mutually exclusive: two sides of the same coin."

Jamie was even more confused. But he didn't want to seem weak minded or mentally incontinent, so he nodded earnestly. "The yin and the yang."

The professor continued, "Think of it like this. You and I are embedded personas in the text of this restaurant. Do you think this table is real?"

"Yes?" Jamie knew well that all was dubitable as far as philosophy was concerned.

"No. It is a mere collection of text. Scientists encourage us to believe that it's made of molecules, but what are molecules? They are descriptions of phenomena. They are text."

"So, the table isn't real. Does that mean that everything is fictive-real? Everything is text."

"Have you ever heard of Heisenberg's Uncertainty Principle?"

"No."

"Well according to this theory you can not accurately know both the velocity and the position of a subatomic particle at the same time. That is exactly the same as the fictive-real and the real-fictive."

Jamie found Professor Swinecraft's knowledge

impressive. "Very interesting. So, we might be participating in the real-fictive or the fictive-real. We aren't really sure."

"Yes and no. You and I could be characters in a text written by an invisible hand."

"Like God?"

"I prefer the more neutral term Prime Author."

"But doesn't this mean that everything is predetermined? That freedom is an illusion?"

"I believe that the Prime Author isn't always busy writing. Most writer's are lazy by nature. Did you know that Earnest Hemingway couldn't have been bothered to change his underwear. It is said that he actually wore the same pair for 15 years. It is also a well established fact that Mr. Hemingway was not an illustrious wiper, if you know what I mean. Can you imagine the stench? That, young man, is pure sloth."

"So, when the Prime Author isn't writing we are free to do what we want?"

"Exactly. When he isn't writing we are very much participating in the real-fictive. When he is writing then it is the fictive-real."

Jamie felt dizzy and had trouble keeping the fictive-real and real-fictive straight.

"We just don't know when the Prime Author is writing and when he isn't."

"Ah, most people don't, but I have discovered a way to know."

*****

Slowpoke Joe and Slim Whitback returned to the

Harvey Dickslop Saloon. The sun was setting and the sky was orange with a touch of red. They went inside the bar and found the same filthy cowhands drunkenly dealing cards for a game of black jack.

"Do you 'member me?" asked Slim.

"Nope," said the bartender pretending that he didn't remember Slim from the day before.

"You're sure you don 'member me? I was here yesterday."

The bartender looked Slim Whitback up and down. "No, I can't say I do."

"I'm the guy lookin for Harvey Dickslop."

"Ah, now I member. This time you brought a friend. An injun friend," said the bartender.

"That's right, mister," said Slim.

Slowpoke Joe put his hand on his six shooter and said, "We look for missing white woman."

The cowhands all sneered and snickered.

"Well, I've seen a whole lot of white women. Maybe you can describe this here woman you're lookin for?"

Slim wasn't the type of cowboy that wasted time, "Well she's got these really purty and dainty feet. All her toes are exactly the same damn size. I ain't never seen nothin like it."

One of the cowhands volunteered, "I once seen a woman with real big feet and her middle toe was bigger than all her other toes."

Another offered, "And I seen a woman with really big fat toes but she ain't got no toe nails."

"Well, I can't say I'm a connoisseur of women's feet,"

said the bartender. "In my business, I don't see many feet anyhow. Most women I know wear some sort a boots or shoes."

"Unless you get real cozy with a woman," chuckled another cowhand.

Slowpoke Joe couldn't believe the bar room chat about feet. "This woman have hair the color of corn husks in Autumn. Her eyes like two small pools where I swim as child in Black Snake river."

"What the hell's he goin on about?" asked the bartender.

The cowhands were getting restless and the bartender expressed his dissatisfaction about the presence of Slowpoke Joe and Slim Whitback. "Maybe you should go see Sluggy Whisper. He sells woman's footwear and whatnot," he suggested trying his hardest to get rid of the two men without a scuffle.

"We know you Harvey Dickslop," blurted Joe pulling his pistol from his holster.

"Well, there ain't no need for vi-o-lence," said the bartender reaching under the counter of the bar for his rifle.

Soon there was a bloody gun fight with the bullets going this way and that. Cowhands bit the dust. Whiskey bottles were shot off shelves. The mirror behind the bar shattered into a million bits. Glass was everywhere. When the shooting stopped, Joe and Slim stood in a puddle of blood. They walked behind the bar and the bartender was gone. He had slipped out like a rat and he had taken with him the whereabouts of Aphrodite Blosom.

(Jamie Dropping embeds himself as Slowpoke Joe (Bloody Boots Buried in the Sand, p.158))

*****

"Do you want to hear something amazing?"

"Sure."

Professor Swinecraft pulled what looked like a small tape recorder from his short sleeved suit coat pocket. He gave Jamie a pair of earphones.

"This device records what ghost chasers call an EVP. Electronic Voice Phenomena. It is a special device that records sounds that are outside of our range of hearing. Listen closely."

Jamie put the ear phones in his ears and listened intently. He didn't know what to expect but he assumed there would be a voice or something like a voice. He closed eyes and listened to silence.

"Did you hear it?"

"What?"

"Listen again." Professor Swinecarft replayed the recording.

Jamie listened.

"I hear some clicking."

"Exactly. But what kind of clicking?"

"I'm not sure."

"It is the sound, of a typewriter. Not just any typewriter though. It is *the* typewriter. It is the Prime Author at work. I've got thousands of hours of tape just like this. This is proof, not only that the Prime Author exists, but the sound of clicking keys means that the Prime Author is working. But there are great periods of silence, where one can only imagine that the Prime Author is on a drinking binge, pleasuring himself in some den of iniquity or perhaps just participating in some unrighteous sloth."

"Incredible."

*****

Jamie Dropping finds Thurme Swinecraft amazing. His intellect is an explosion of light. A pure genius. Thurme Swinecraft with his enormous testicles, dark bags under his eyes, wispy white hair, overgrown eyebrows, hair spilling out of his ears, large pores and oily monstrous nose is nothing short of brilliant.

What Jamie does not know, but what is important to our story is that Thurme Swinecraft had once loved a woman but she left him when she realized that he was already engaged to the Embedded Persona. But that was a long, long time ago. Now the Professor spends his afternoons in his lonely living room watching TV and usually eating microwavable meals. Post Embedded Persona, the formula of Thurme Swinecraft's life is macaroni and cheese, canned laughter and coerced applause. Today, as the Prime Author would have it, he had decided to go out for a quick bite to eat.

*****

Thurme Swinecraft pulled a fork and knife from an interior pocket of his short sleeved suit coat and plunged the knife into his hamburger.

"Professor Swinecraft, I know that you are retired, but maybe you could help me...mentor me. You could help me understand the theory better."

"With   your   choice   of   book...Bloody   Boobs   or

whatever it's called...I think you should stick with Lacan or perhaps Derrida."

"Maybe you could help me find a better book?"

"Hmmm. It is something I could think about."

"Fantastic."

"Would you mind getting me some more water, please?"

Jamie raced back to the kitchen and announced to the cook and dishwasher, "You won't believe who is here..."

"Another asshole who wants a cheeseburger without cheese?" yawned the dishwasher.

"Professor Thurme Swinecraft."

"Who the hell is he?"

"The man responsible for the theory of the Embedded Persona?"

"Sounds like a real asshole."

"He's absolutely brilliant..he's just delivered a lecture about the fictive-real...we are text...everything is text...absolutely brilliant." Jamie quickly took a fresh *glass* pitcher full of water back to the dining room.

He poured a glass for the professor..

"This is a very disappointing cheeseburger without cheese."

"Would you like me to get you something else?"

"No, just the check please."

Jamie prepared the bill and went back to the table. $6.70

"So, Professor Swinecraft, will you help me?"

"I have given it some thought and my answer is no."

"No?"

"No."

"Why professor? We could maybe meet just a couple of times..."

"No. I think it is for the best. My doctor has told me that I should put the theory away. Maybe he is right. I have to admit, meeting you and having this discussion has been wonderful. It is good to see that I have defeated that baboon Polygoat. It is wonderful to see that my theory, that my ideas have endured. But I don't have the energy anymore. You must understand, young man, that theory had nearly destroyed me. While I labored on that theory, I paid attention to nothing else. Nothing else mattered. So much of my life was lived and I noticed none of it. " Here the professor stopped and just stared vacantly. Then he continued, "I once was in...there was this woman..." he paused and collected himself, "My cat, Jasper, my life long companion died while I was busy chasing papers. I was even too busy to give him a proper burial. I pitched his dead body in the garbage. Can you imagine that? It is time to put the embedded persona away. I hope you understand, but no, I cannot help you."

Professor Swinecraft stood up and pulled seven dollars from his wallet. He sighed, "You can keep the change."

Thirty cents and a sigh.

*****

And now we are at the end. Jamie Dropping watches Professor Thurme Swinecraft hobble out of the restaurant and into the suburban dusk with its sighing blues and yawning reds. Is he disappointed? Immensely. Did he take the rejection personally? Yes. As the door closes, Jamie Dropping goes back to his book. He begins to re-read the pages describing the fictive-real and the real-fictive. But as he reads he doesn't think about the words on the page. The words don't even reach him. He is preoccupied with thoughts of the yin and the yang, plastic molecule decay, cheeseburgers without cheese, short sleeved suit coats, Electronic Voice Phenomena, the Prime Author, Dr. Polygoat, Heisenberg and his Principle of Uncertainty ...

He puts the book aside, goes to the window and watches the people walking by. He sees Professor Swinecraft hobbling his way across the street and thinks, "What an amazing mind."

The radio in the kitchen plays the song *El Paso* by Marty Robbins.

*****

Slim Whitback rode out of town on his trusty steed Sparky. The sun was setting and Slim had a long way to travel until he reached the next town named Black Hatchet.

The sky was orange with a touch of scarlet. He took Aphrodite's boots that he found buried in the sand and held them tenderly in his arms. Her white boots embossed with little golden stars. He began to weep.

Sparky gave a nagging neigh. The steed was impatient to get out of town.

"Ah, Sparky I've got some dirt in my eyes. That's all," wept Slim. "We found Aphrodite's boots, so she has to be out there somewhere, bootless in the world."

He gave Sparky a limp kick and a half hearted "giddy up." Sparky neighed and stood on his hind legs. And then they were gone.

All that Slim had were a pair of Bloody boots that he had found buried not far from town. Slim knew it was a sign left for him by Aphrodite. She had left more than her footsteps, she had left her bloody boots buried in the sand.

(*Bloody Boots Buried in the Sand, p.156*)

THE UNEMPLOYABLES

J amie Dropping had some issues. His wife's ghost haunted him; he was certain that he was being secretly investigated by the police; and now he had lost his job.

His therapist had told him that losing his job was a chance to reincarnate himself. It was a new beginning. Then she gave him a long lecture about the *Tibetan Book of the Dead*. "Just before the soul of dead person is recycled and reborn in a new body, the soul has the ability to choose which womb-door to re-enter life through. Choosing the womb-door is critical: it is the difference between being reborn a human or a tapeworm."

Jamie found the whole womb-door theory a real bummer. He was expecting sympathy from his therapist, even false sympathy. But instead he had to settle for the womb-door. His therapist instructed with bubblegum exuberance, "All you need to do is find your womb-door."

All the talk about wombs and entry and re-entry began to make Jamie feel slightly uncomfortable. His palms were sweaty and his mouth tasted chalky. He even began to wonder if the womb-door was therapist code for sex. Maybe this was the way psychoanalysts flirted with their patients. Maybe it was an invitation? Maybe it was a test?

But Jamie found his therapist repulsive. She had a body like Hefty garbage bag filled with grass clippings. She rarely smiled but when she did, she displayed a mouthful of brown uneven teeth. She wore thick glasses that made her eyes seem like enormous insect eyes. But worst of all was her hair. Her hair always looked as if it had just landed on her head after flying across the Atlantic. While his therapist talked about womb-doors, much to Jamie's chagrin, his imagination began to play a film featuring him and his therapist engaged in an awkward and lusty act of fornication. Jamie cringed. He tried to censor the onslaught of images by reciting the alphabet in reverse. That didn't work, so he began to ponder baseball statistics. He thought about lint and socks, parking meters, anything completely asexual. But nothing worked. By the end of the session, he was imagining himself in nothing but a pair of socks, licking the lint out of his therapist's belly button while she was leaning against a parking meter.

On his drive home, Jamie concluded he definitely needed a new analyst. Someone a little less interested in eastern metaphysics.

*****

As fate would have it, a couple sessions later, Jamie's therapist cut the cord. Because he had no job, and money was tight, he had asked her if he could pay for therapy once he found work.

She thought about this for a long silent moment. "Are you looking for a job?" she asked.

"Of course," he lied.

She was pensive. "Something gives me the impression that you aren't really interested in finding your womb-door. Is that true?"

"Well, I have to admit I'm a bit confused about the whole womb-door thing."

"What are you confused about?"

Jamie really hadn't given much serious thought to the idea of a womb-door. But he had absentmindedly wondered if the whole womb-door concept was behind the sitcom *Gilligan's Island*. He explained his theory, "Every episode begins with the hope of rebirth – a plan to escape from the uncharted island – and every episode ends with the collapse of their plans because Gilligan would bumble the deal. It seems that the message of the show is, *Don't find your womb-door. Stay lost at sea.*"

Jamie's therapist considered *Gilligan's Island* a travesty of American Culture. It, like all sitcoms, demonstrated the septic tank depth of the average American's IQ. She said with venomous condescension, "I don't understand what a 1960's sitcom about a boob named Gilligan has to do with you and your womb-door."

She had now used the words *boob* and *womb* in the same sentence. Jamie's immigration fired-up the projector. Soon there was another flood of stomach turning sex scenes. Jamie looked away and said, "Do you want to have sex with me?"

His therapist was pensive again. Jamie could never read what she was thinking. She always had a black and white rorschach look in her eyes.

Her gaze directed Jamie's attention to a painting hanging from the wall adjacent to her desk. He had *seen* this painting in a thousand therapy sessions. A watercolor of a butterfly. But now he *really* saw it. He suddenly realized it was not the insect paradigm of metamorphosis. It was actually a vagina. The womb.

"You know, I don't think I'll be able to help you any longer," said the therapist – barely opening her mouth as she spoke.

Jamie squinted at the picture, to get a better look. Maybe it was just a cave.

And that was his last session.

*****

Jamie Dropping, besides being jobless, was now an analysand without an analyst, which made him feel like a stray dog soaked from a terrifying thunder storm, like a shopping cart abandoned in a vacant lot. He felt directionless, a million miles from home. Lost.

He spent his waking hours in brutal self-examination. He revisited his past, pulled the skeletons from his closets and interrogated his former selves for some sort of solace, for an explanation. He just wanted to be happy being Jamie Dropping. But the only truth he was able to unearth was that he was a failure. A loser.

Someone without any redeeming quality. A schlemiel. A rube. He perpetrated his own failure.

Jamie then decided that he had enough. Thinking exhausted him, and surviving was killing him. He was not the type who could slit his wrists or hang himself. He had no choice but to hang-on. But hanging-on made him feel nauseous. So he squandered his time sitting on the edge of his couch in the living room of his apartment, slightly nauseous, the curtains drawn. He would sit in the darkness, remote control in hand, and he would watch TV. It rained its images on Jamie Dropping and his waking hours were washed away with canned laughter and phony applause: *Happy Days*, *The Andy Griffith Show*, *The Beverly Hillbillies*, *The Jeffersons*, *Gilligan's Island*, *Different Strokes*, *Family Ties*, *Threes Company*, *The Munsters*, *Sanford and Son*, *The Adams Family*, *Mr. Ed*, *The Brady Bunch*, *Bewitched*, *I Dream of Jeannie*, *I Love Lucy*, *Leave it to Beaver*, *My Three Sons*...

He watched and thought vaguely about the womb-door. He knew full well that Gilligan and Skipper would never find their womb-door. Lucy and Ethel, the Beaver, Richie Cunningham, George Jefferson, Jethro, and all the others, were all looking for their womb-doors, but the Law of the half-hour American sitcom was very clear: finding the womb-door is not good comedy.

*****

One day Jamie's only friend, Howard Strangula, called him. Howard and Jamie had been friends since high school, although Jamie never really liked Howard at all. He considered Howard an emotional leech and tolerated his random interruptions in his life as existential flat tires.

Howard Strangula was also jobless, but unlike Jamie, he wasn't whittling his existence away watching reruns and pining for his womb-door. Howard was an entrepreneur. Sure, he was lazy, but in an ambitious way. "I want to talk to you about this great business venture," he told Jamie.

"What is it?" Jamie could smell a pyramid scheme through the phone.

"Well, I don't want to talk about it over the phone. You never know who's listening."

"Didn't you call me to talk about it?"

"I just wanted to tell you we should talk about it. But not now. Not over the phone."

"I really don't think anyone is listening," Jamie didn't even want to be part of the conversation.

"Don't you remember what happened to Billy Murdel?"

"Billy Murdel?" the name was vaguely familiar.

"From high school. You don't remember Billy Murdel?"

"No."

"Come on. The real loser. The red haired kid with braces."

"Billy Murdel?" Jamie recalled a kid with red hair and braces. "You mean the kid with the knobby knees who always smelled like a gas station?"

"Could've been. I don't usually look at boys knees. Anyway, he was talking on the phone about someone he shouldn't, and the next day he found his testicles in the freezer."

"What do you mean he found his testicles in the freezer?"

"He found his testicles in the freezer," repeated Howard.

"So, one day Billy Murdel went to get some ice-cubes and he said, 'Oh look there are my testicles.' Don't you think he would have realized before he opened the freezer that his testicles were missing?"

Howard sighed, "We shouldn't be talking about this over the phone."

Jamie closed his eyes and took a couple of deep breaths. Talking to Howard was always an infuriating business. Then he asked, "Howard, why do you call me to talk about things you can't talk about over the phone?"

Howard cleared his throat and said in complete monotone, "I'm inviting you into a dialogue, Jamie. Come over to my place tomorrow and we can talk it over. That's all."

******

The next day, Jamie reluctantly set off for Howard's apartment. He was far from his psychological best. He felt nauseous and the whole ordeal of driving seemed like an enormous illogical hassle. Stop signs, traffic, red lights, yellow lights, green lights, flashing yellow lights, dotted lines, solid lines, turn signals, turning lanes, windshield wipers were all part of a sadistic plot invented solely to torture him. He just wanted to sit in his living room and watch *Gilligan's Island*.

But Jamie could never say *No* to Howard and for some reason always obediently did whatever Howard wanted him to do. Jamie cursed himself for being such a coward as he slid the key into the ignition. Why couldn't he just tell Howard to go screw himself? Why did he always do the things that made him miserable?

Jamie drove cautiously. He didn't exceed 32 miles per hour even though the speed limit was 45. Behind him was a long line of impatient traffic. Every driver and passenger stuck in that line was irritated by the subnormally slow speed. Behind Jamie was an old man driving a beat up 1976 Dodge Eris. He rode Jamie's ass and honked viciously. Jamie could see the old man in his rear view mirror. He had stringy grey hair, blown wild by the wind. He was giving Jamie the finger and screaming at him, although Jamie couldn't hear what he was screaming. He quietly cursed the old man, "I'm not feeling well you old fucker."

Jamie thought old people were a nuisance, but old people that putted around impatiently trying to get somewhere before the end were pathetic. They had wasted all their lives, and now in the waning years they were in a hurry to get to the pharmacy to buy laxatives. He found it disgusting that the old man didn't simply stay at home watching *The Young and the Restless* until he kicked the bucket.

*****

The whole ten mile drive to Howard's apartment was an epic journey greater than Dante's excursion through hell. As he pulled into Howard's apartment complex he felt like a half dead goldfish floating in the toilet bowl just prior the final flush.

Jamie parked his car and cursed Howard, "GOD DAMNED IDIOT." He hated Howard because he couldn't say *No* to him. It didn't make sense, but that's how he felt. He hated himself for always doing what Howard asked him to do. It was another of his failures: he was a pathetic yes man – a coward, afraid of the word *no*. He sat in the car simmering with self consuming rage.

Jamie also hated Howard because he was always blabbing about his supposedly superior IQ. But Howard had the EQ of a handful of gravel. He talked and talked, but he never listened. He didn't give a damn about what Jamie felt or thought. He just needed something or someone to fill the profound lack in his super-sized ego. Jamie was Howard's "lack-filler," and he knew that Howard didn't empathize with him. Whenever Jamie hung out with Howard, he always felt even more isolated and alone. And that's why Jamie really hated Howard.

*****

Jamie dragged his feet to Howard's apartment building and rang the buzzer.

"Who is it?" crackled a voice from the intercom.

Jamie said nothing. He frowned bitterly and pressed the buzzer again violently, imagining that he was shoving his thumb into one of Howard's eyes.

The door clicked open and Jamie marched up the stairs to Howard's apartment. The door was open, and Howard was standing in the doorway, wearing a shirt that read, *No Work, No School, No Problem!* The shirt was small and it didn't completely cover Howard's gut. It ended just prior to his hairy bellybutton. Jamie was disgusted by the sight of it.

"Hi Jamie," said Howard.

"So, what's your stupid business plan," snapped Jamie.

"I've got a great plan," bubbled Howard.

*****

Before going into the plan, Howard asked if Jamie wanted a cup of coffee which he declined with the wave of a hand. Howard sipped at his coffee, making loud slurping noises. Jamie sank into the couch and stared at the ceiling.

"You know what I've been doing?"

Jamie said nothing.

"I've been spending a lot of time looking for the missing me."

"Great."

"I've relocated a lot of people who were important to me. I've found all my high school friends on Facebook. I began to get nostalgic for the good ol' days. You know, the glory days. That's why I dug this shirt out of storage. What do you think?"

Glory days? Howard, obviously had a strange understanding of the word *glory*. Unless Howard thought being duct taped in the shower of the boys locker room was a glorious experience. Howard had obviously forgotten that they were picked on relentlessly in high school.

"So, I've been chatting with the guys from high

school every now and then. Did you know that Jorge Powers is an actor and he played the transvestite in the movie *The Sludge Factory*?"

The idea that Jorge Powers had managed to succeed, if playing the part of a transvestite could be counted as success, made Jamie feel like an insect scuttling across the filth and dirt of his own failure. He felt buried beneath a lifetime of loserdom. How in the hell had Jorge Powers managed to become anything? Jamie hated Jorge Powers even more than he had when they were both in high school.

"So you probably want to see my business plan?"

"Oh, yeah," yawned Jamie.

Howard raced to the bedroom and closed the door.

While Jamie waited on the couch, his thoughts were flaming arrows all fired at Howard. Howard had reached a new all time low. Jamie was on a quest for his womb-door, a chance of rebirth and reincarnation while Howard was clinging to a previous incarnation of himself from a humiliating acne-faced-smelly-armpitted period known as high school.

"Are you friends with Billy Murdel?" Jamie shouted to Howard.

"No. The bastard hasn't accepted my friend request."

Billy Murdel, thought Jamie. He closed his eyes and pulled Billy's face from his mind. Red hair. Thin as a rail. Braces. Acne. Dandruff. He was picked on all the time. There was a linebacker named Blane Dongle that made it his daily duty to terrorize and embarrass Billy Murdel.

Jamie sighed, *What the hell is taking Howard so long?* He wondered. Then he closed his eyes and he drifted back to high school.

He revisited the sloppy stench of the cafeteria and a couple of insipid classrooms. The faces of the boys that traumatized him, and the girls that ridiculed him for no good reason, came in and out of focus. He saw the girls that he adored, but never had the courage to speak to, fluttering in the hallways. Missed opportunities. Then he found himself in the sultry armpit of the boys locker room quickly pulling on his jock strap before any of the other boys could see his dick.

*****

"So what do you think?" asked Howard.

Jamie opened his eyes and saw Howard standing in front of him wearing an enormous refrigerator box that had been spray painted silver. The box had some blue knobs and red buttons glued in random groups on the front of it. Howard's face was also painted silver and it protruded from a hole in the front of the box, and two holes were cut into the sides for his arms.

"Hello little boy would you like to shake hands with Roborob?" Howard spoke and moved mechanically. He stuck his hand out for Jamie to shake.

Jamie recoiled and asked, "What the hell is this?"

"I'm a robot. I stand outside the science center. The kids really go for this type of crap. It's a great gig."

"You want me to dress up like a robot?" Jamie began to feel faint.

"No. I want you take the photos." Howard clumsily maneuvered through his living room, knocking into furniture, looking for his Polaroid camera. He found it buried beneath some bills and coupons. He handed it to Jamie.

"Sometimes parents give me a buck or some pocket change for letting them take a picture of their kid standing next to me. But, if you take the photos, then I can charge a couple of bucks for each one. They get a souvenir and our profits are up 150%. Everyone's happy," Howard effervesced.

"*Our* profits?"

"Believe me we can make a shitload doing this. And we'll split everything sixty forty. What do you think?"

Jamie understood he was the forty of the equation. "It sounds awful."

"Listen, don't decide anything now, just come out with me today and then make your decision."

"This is an awful idea," Jamie echoed. But he couldn't say *no*.

****

Jamie didn't have the psychological stamina to get behind the wheel and the drive to science center, so Howard volunteered to drive. But before going downtown he wanted to make a stop at the party store for some "refreshments."

Jamie waited in the car. He stared out the window thinking about the different ways in which people committed suicide. He thought about the people from his grandfather's generation who would jump off bridges.

Drowning seemed so barbaric. Suicide required a type of bravery that Jamie did not possess.

He saw Howard standing at the cash register and his mind drifted to murder. Maybe he could murder Howard in some way that made it look like an accident. He wondered if he could convince the police that Howard had driven over himself accidentally.

Howard returned with two cans of beer. "I usually have a beer. It helps calm the nerves. And check this out." Howard pulled out a pack of straws and a couple of rubbery can sleeves that had Pepsi written on them from the glove box. "This way it doesn't look like we're drinking beers. It looks like we're drinking pop."

"It's against the law to drink in public." Jamie didn't bring up the fact that it was only 9:30 in the morning.

"That's the whole point. With our beer disguise kits, no one would ever suspect that we're drinking."

"Beer disguise kits?"

"Do you think Donald Trump can't drink wherever the hell he wants?"

"We aren't Donald Trump."

"Not yet."

Howard smiled. Jamie frowned.

*****

The rest of the drive, Jamie suffered Howard's ridiculous theory of the letter aitch. Howard was excited and when he was excited he became garrulous.

"You know, one day, I suddenly realized that the building where I worked was shaped like an enormous **H**. The **aitch,** Jamie: two legs connected by a bridge, beginning just past the **G** with H–Bomb and ending prior to the **I** with hysterics. It's not a good letter."

Jamie sighed and rolled his eyes. Howard had obviously been rehearsing this little speech.

"Ah the **aitch** – articulated with the epiglottis against the back of the pharynx – the voiceless breath of the letter **aitch**. It is a seemingly innocent letter, as are most letters, with the exception of the **double-u**, but in the mouths and minds of the wicked it can be a letter of cruel design."

"What the hell are you talking about?"

"I once saw an episode of the Hugh Proton Show about the Antichrist. One of the guest panelists claimed that the letter **aitch** was the Antichrist. This guy said that the letter **aitch** was actually the brains behind John Hinckley's attempted assassination of Ronald Wilson Reagan."

"Oh, for the love of God. How can a letter be the Antichrist?"

Howard ignored the question, "And the **aitch** was also the address of the cellblock where some of the worst female criminals in the history of Australian Television spent their 692 episodes of life. *Prisoner: Cell Block H.* Don't tell me you never watched *Cell Bock H.*"

Jamie couldn't believe the stupidity of the monologue. He sulked and stared out the window. He imagined that a giant letter *H* was terrorizing the streets of downtown. Stepping on families that didn't have enough sense to stay off the streets. It was *Sesame Street* meets Sam Peckinpah; the Cookie Monster, Bert and Ernie,

Grover, Kermit all being crushed by the letter aitch.

*****

Howard couldn't find a parking spot near the science center, and he didn't want to spend any money on parking, so they circled and circled the science center, hunting for a spot. Jamie was ready to strangle Howard on the third go-round.

"What makes you think you're going to find a spot, this time? Why don't we just park in the parking lot?"

"I'm not going to pay to park."

Howard suddenly saw a car pull out of a spot. He pulled in, but it was a handicapped spot.

"You can't park here," sighed Jamie.

"Who say's I can't park here?"

"It's a handicapped spot."

"Have you ever seen a handicapped person in the science center?"

"The last time I was at the science center I think I was ten."

Howard continued, "And that guy that just pulled out, was he handicapped?"

Jamie hadn't paid much attention to the car leaving. "How would I know?"

"Well, he wasn't unless hemorrhoids is a handicap."

*****

As they exited Howard's air conditioned car, Jamie suddenly recalled why he hated downtown. He always found it oppressively hot, even in the winter. Hell had to be cooler. He looked into the sky and squinted. The sun was somewhere up there but it was impossible to tell where. It was obscured behind a hazy wall of miserable silver clouds.

Howard marched in the direction of the science center, carrying a small bag and dragging the enormous silver box. Jamie followed at a distance.

"Jamie, we are the chosen few. We no longer have to spend our lives doing some job we hate. You and me are free men. Free from the office and from the computer. Free from emails. Free from boss' that have their heads up their asses..."

Howard stopped at a small grassy patch just outside the science center. "This...this Jamie, is my new office. This is where Roborob comes to life. Hey, lets have a drink to celebrate."

Howard cracked his beer and took a suck through the straw. Jamie did the same. He didn't want any beer but he figured it was easier to just drink it rather than argue with Howard about drinking beer in public. Jamie took a long drink through the straw.

Howard put out an empty Maxwell House Coffee can. He dropped a couple dollars in the can and some change. "Do you have a couple bucks for the can? People are more likely to give money when they believe someone else has already given. No one wants to be first. It's psychological."

Jamie reached into his pocket. He had exactly 2 dollars and 78 cents. He put a nickel into the can.

"During the week things can be pretty slow, but the security guard inside, Juan, he tips me off. He told me that there would be a field trip today. If you play a field trip right, it can be a goldmine."

Howard put on the box.

"Now you're a shark. Don't loiter around with the camera, just wait. Once you see the kids around me you attack. Take a picture and try to give it to one of the kids. That's the key. Make sure they take the photo. If you put the photo in their hands – they'll most likely buy it because they want to be left alone. It's that simple."

******

Howard prepared himself. He put on the silver box, did some deep breathing exercises and then asked Jamie to give him another sip from his "soda." Jamie reluctantly held the straw up to Howard's lips so he could take a drink. Then, Howard stood perfectly still.

Some people in a hurry to get to work filed past, taking no notice of him. Jamie stood a good 20 feet away from him near a park bench where a flock of little old ladies were throwing out bird seed for some pigeons. One of the pigeons climbed on his shoe and took a shit.

A school bus arrived and a swarm of children exited. They were screaming and shouting. Jamie disliked children more than old people. He looked at them as if they were a bunch of runny nosed, budding neuroses. Sociopaths in training. Although Jamie had no idea what age this group of children were, he assumed that they were only a few years away from diapers. Disgusting. The kids ran to Howard, and he started to move his arms up and down mechanically.

"Hello kids, my name is Roborob."

"Look! A robot," shouted a chorus of kids who all

~177~

shared the same subnormal intellect.

"It's just a man dressed like a robot," said a skinny little girl with a black eye patch covering one eye.

The teacher stumbled from the bus. She looked frazzled. She tried to count the kids as they jumped around Howard and gave up after a few attempts. A couple of parents accompanying the class field trip also exited the bus behind the teacher.

The teacher pulled her camera from her purse. "OK class, everyone gather around the robot and I'll take a picture."

"No pictures please. I have my own cameraman. Only $2.00 for a photo," Jamie arrived on cue and limply displayed the Polaroid camera to the teacher.

She looked at Jamie as if he was trying to peddle his soiled underwear. "It's OK. I'll take a picture myself."

"Listen lady. You need to pay for the photo," said Howard.

"It's just one photo for the classroom," insisted the teacher

"No money, no photo," said Howard breaking the so-called fourth wall and talking like Howard Strangula.

"Listen, I'll just take a photo. It's only two dollars," Jamie sniveled diplomatically.

"I'm not going to pay for a photograph," she snapped.

Howard turned his back to the teacher as she was getting ready to take a photo. "NO MONEY, NO FUCKING PHOTO."

All the kids oohed and awed when they heard the

word *fuck*.

"Fine. Kids, come on Mr. Robot is being a real jerk."

The kids dispersed slowly. One of them, a chubby little kid with untied shoelaces tripped and knocked over Howard's disguised beer.

"God damn it. Watch where you're going you little retard."

Then one of the chaperones, a father with broad shoulders and muscular arms stepped forward, "Hey Robo Dork! I don't like the way you talked to the kids or the teacher."

Howard looked the father in the face and spat, "Listen Chumly, that clumsy little fucker kicked over my..."

Howard stopped and gave the father a closer look, "Are you Billy Murdel?"

The father was surprised. He looked closely at Howard. Howard gazed deeply into the other man's eyes. It was like two dogs meeting on the street, each sniffing the other's ass.

"Are you Howard Strangula?" asked the father.

"Billy you've really changed," said Howard.

"Exquese me," it was the other chaperone, a mother dressed for a funeral, "but I don like da langigde you been usin in da front of da chilren."

"What language would that be lady, English?" Howard chuckled and nudged Billy Murdel with his elbow, winking at him.

The mother gasped, "You da trashbin of da u ess a."

Hearing the name Billy Murdel, Jamie wandered over

to get a look at him. Billy had in fact changed. He looked good. Healthy and fit. He was no longer the wedgified high school loser he once was.

"Billy, it's great to see you. Sorry to hear about your...ahem..." Jamie leaned closer to Billy and said, "testicles."

The mother overheard the word *testicles* and gasped again. She looked at Billy Murdel, "Why dees men talk to you abut you privarts?"

Billy Murdel tried to smile, "Listen you two are really beginning to piss me off. You were complete morons in high school and look at you now: dressed up like robots, picking on third graders and drinking beers with straws."

A small mob of onlookers began to gather around Jamie, Howard, Billy and the mother.

Jamie was shocked that Billy felt they were morons. He felt betrayed. They had all shared the same high school status. Once upon a time, they were all losers. Back then Billy was just as big a moron as they were.

Howard sensed that Billy seemed insulted about something, and he didn't understand if it was something he had said or done, so he asked, "Hey man, is she your ball and chain?"

"You want me to introduce you to my ball and chain?" Billy Murdel made a fist. "This is my ball." He pointed at his bicep, "This is my chain."

"Why are you talking like that Billy? Are you dating a professional wrestler or something?" Howard asked.

Suddenly, towards the back of the mob, Jamie saw

the face of his therapist. He saw her clearly, her face bobbed between the heads of others. It was an omen. His heart stopped. All of reality went mute. Words stopped making sound. He could hear nothing but the sound of his own heart beating. Then her face was gone.

Jamie craned his neck and searched the crowd for his therapist. He felt desperate. He jumped up and down, searching for her.

"What the hell is wrong with him?" Billy Murdel asked Howard.

"Dr. Veronica, I'm looking for my womb-door," Jamie shouted. The crowd collectively gasped. "I swear to God. This is just an experiment...I'm looking for..." Jamie fell to his knees and nearly sobbed. "...MY...WOMB...DOOR. I really am."

There was a moment of baffled silence. Then the mother dressed in black asked, "Why dis man scream for woom? You da trashbin of u ess a." Then, she actually spat on the back of Jamie's head.

"I'm not gonna let some bitch spit on my..." Howard didn't know what hit him. Billy punched him with such force that his fist broke through the spray painted cardboard and hit Howard on his sternum and knocked him off his feet and onto his ass.

While Howard was on the ground, the mother hit him on the face with her black raven shaped purse. His nose started to bleed. Seeing blood, Jamie shrieked.

Some people in the mob, who couldn't see all the action, saw some blood flying and thought that Howard had hit the woman. "That son of a bitch dressed up like a robot hit that poor lady," said one onlooker. Another person shouted out, "The robot's buddy was screaming about that poor ladies pussy." Statements like this were heard by others and soon some civic minded citizens decided that they needed to defend the defenseless. Soon the whole mob was buzzing with violence.

As the crowd began to tumble on top of Jamie and Howard, Jamie decided that he needed to get the hell out of there. He tried to push his way through the crowd, but they pushed him back. The onlookers jeered, bit, kicked, punched and spat on him as he tried to break free. Escape was impossible.

Jamie didn't give up, though. He got back on his feet, wiped the saliva from his face, lowered his shoulder and pushed his way into the crowd. But to no avail. He tried again. Still nothing. Then again. This time he was met by the same stubborn mass of the mob, but there was a strange force that seemed to push Jamie. It was like the whole mob contracted and Jamie was shot out. He got to his feet, looked around in bewilderment and ran.

*****

Jamie hid behind Howard's car. He ducked behind it and peeked over the tail light hoping for a sign of Howard.

Twenty minutes later Howard arrived. He staggered to his car, nose bleeding, face bruised. The box had gaping holes everywhere, only a few blue knobs and red buttons remained in place. The others had been ripped off.

Jamie, still hiding behind the back of the car, whispered. "Howard, are you OK?"

Howard said nothing. He struggled painfully to remove the box. He threw it on the ground and kicked it. Then he unlocked the car. He stood there panting for a moment, and with every heave of his chest his belly button peeked out from the bottom of his shirt. *No Work, No School, No Problem !*

*****

On the ride home, neither Jamie nor Howard had much to say. Howard stared in front him, his knuckles were white from wringing the steering wheel as he drove. He was angry that his nearly virtual friendship with Billy Murdel came to such an abrupt and violent end, and he blamed Jamie for the whole riot.

"Why the hell did you talk to Billy Murdel about his testicles?" Howard snapped the silence.

"You told me they were missing."

"You just can't go up to a man and ask him about his testicles."

Jamie said nothing.

"And what was all that bullshit about the womb?"

"I'm looking for my womb-door," mumbled Jamie.

"What the fuck is a womb-door?"

Jamie didn't care to explain. He sensed that Howard really wasn't interested anyway.

As they drove back to Howard's apartment, Jamie stared out the window, not really looking at anything in particular. He was asphyxiated by what he felt, which he really didn't know how to put into words. After a while of marinating in his own numbness, he closed his eyes.

Howard mumbled, "I can't fucking believe it."

*****

While they drove, Jamie's thoughts led him to his high school. For some reason, he remembered a memory that had always stuck with him. When he had been a sophomore, his cross country coach had told him, "You could be a good runner if you just put on your shoes and ran." Maybe the coach had been right. Maybe Jamie's problem was that he just didn't try hard enough. He didn't push himself. He lacked drive and ambition. Discipline. He lacked discipline.

He sighed and began to wonder about his womb-door. Maybe it would solve all his problems. But what could he do to find it? Was it even out there? If so, how would he recognize it?

Jamie vowed, he would no longer be a Gilligan stranded on a deserted island. He would find his way home again. He would break free from his couch and his soft, boring life. He would live again. He felt suddenly relieved. Everything would be all right. He just didn't know where to begin. And if there was one thing Jamie knew, it was that beginnings were always more difficult than endings.

*****

As they drove, and as Howard muttered to himself, the clouds in the sky parted revealing a strip of blue sky. The sun even seemed to wink at Jamie from behind a grey cloud.

THIS TIME THE WORLD REALLY IS ENDING AGAIN

The whole country was going ape shit for the end of the world. Comets, aliens, wars, diseases, natural disasters, fascist state conspiracy freakouts. It's all people talked about. Newspapers, television, the Internet – it was one gigantic shit storm that smelled worse than a port-o-john at a Megadeth concert. One thing seemed certain, everyone was jonesing for the final scene. Even the Government was making foreign policy decisions based on the prophecies of Nostradamus. Everyone was bucking for the end.

And then there was Jamie Dropping. He wasn't particularly interested in all the hype about the world ending. He had his own problems to deal with. He no longer felt the warm embers of happiness. Life for Jamie was a lot of smoke with very little flame. Now that he was nearing the age of retirement, he felt his age. He woke up, his ankles hurt. His legs were stiff. Actually his left leg was beyond stiff. It was completely numb. He could sleep for twelve hours and still feel exhausted.

After his shower he would vacantly stare at himself in the bathroom mirror. He saw at the dark bags under his eyes and wondered about his glory years. He had had them. There was a happy idealized past somewhere...He gave up thinking, dried his hair had a quick cup of coffee and hit the road. Off to work. Another shitty day.

As the world was ending (again), Jamie's numb leg began to worry him. It had happened on a dreary humid evening. Jamie had gone to bed, and when he woke up the next morning his leg had as much feeling as a roll of toilet paper. Like any normal person, Jamie hoped that the numbness would go away just as suddenly as it had appeared. But as the numbness persisted, he began to interpret his leg as a sign: this was the beginning of the end. He had thought about seeing a doctor, but he had soundly reasoned, *What good is a doctor if you're dying?* Of course, Jamie didn't *really* believe he was dying. He rarely even thought seriously about death. Hell death didn't exist; it was something that happened to other people. He still had plenty of time. But it seemed like a good enough excuse to avoid the hassle of a doctor's visit.

Jamie's other problem was occupational. He was a life insurance salesman at a peculiar point in history that the media was calling "the end-of-time." He had been selling life insurance for the last 12 years, and once upon a time he had been moderately successful at it. But now it was near impossible. When the world is ending all the time, it is difficult to see the utility of life insurance. Most people had reasoned, just as soundly as Jamie had reasoned about doctors, *What good is insurance when the world is ending?*

Even though it was a tough market, Jamie was able to sell a policy here and there. His strategy was simple. Every now and then, one of the myriad Doomsday groups would throw an end of the world pep rally. There would be guest speakers, brownies, punch, cheerleaders, sing-a-longs, and, of course, lots of talk about death and dying. Jamie would pose as a new member and try to meet people. He would work the crowd, taking down names and phone numbers. His pitch was, "I'm a new member and I thought it would be cool to meet some other members and really get to know them before the end of the world." Most people looked at Jamie as if he were a hideous freak, but every now and then there was a taker, like Mr. and Mrs. Lint.

Jamie had met Mr. and Mrs. Lint at a rally that celebrated the arrival of time traveling aliens from another dimension. The aliens hadn't arrived yet, but they were rocketing through some other dimension in their Doomsday rockets. Once they landed on earth they were going to blow the shit out of everything and everybody. But the aliens had made contact with the group leader, Dr. Jerry Rammer, and had instructed him to

ORGANIZE AN ARMY. ORGANIZE AN ARMY OF SOLDIERS THAT WILL SERVE AS THE VEHICLES FOR OUR MASS VIOLENCE AND WE WILL REWARD YOU AND YOUR ARMY INFINITELY.

The verb "reward" and the adverb "infinitely" were interpreted by Dr. Rammer to mean that the group would be whisked away to the home of the aliens, which Dr. Rammer said was just east of a planet named Hulga. No one seemed too concerned with the troubling phrase "vehicles for our mass violence."

Mr. and Mrs. Lint were passing out homemade chocolate chip cookies at the end-of-the-world-lets-be-vehicles-of-aliens rally. They were old. Real old. They were well beyond their golden years. Jamie knew they weren't insurable *per se*, but you never could tell. Maybe they had children. Grandchildren.

When Mrs. Lint saw Jamie standing in line with the other Doomers (that's what people were called who waited around for doomsday all the time) waiting for cookies, she told him, "You remind me of my son. Except he's a bit shorter and has longer hair. He doesn't wear glasses. Could you take your glasses off?"

Mrs. Lint had spent a lifetime perfecting the art of false sympathy. She was sweet and kind looking, but behind the silver haired grandmother facade was a cold, calculating misanthrope. Mrs. Lint always pretended to like her son publicly, but in private, he was her Judas.

Jamie took off his glasses and grinned. "Doesn't he look like Chad, Charley?" Charley Lint, was also handing out cookies, but his unhappiness was genuine. "Chad's an idiot."

"Yes, but this man, doesn't he look like Chad?" Mrs. Lint insisted.

Mr. Lint squinted at Jamie for a moment and said, "Chad's taller and he wears glasses."

It was clear that neither Mr. Lint nor Mrs. Lint remembered what their son looked like anymore. It had been a long, long time since they had seen or heard from Chad. It didn't matter. Jamie saw his opportunity, so he popped the question. "Do you think we could hang out and get to know one another before the aliens arrive?"

Mrs. Lint pretended to be pleased with the idea, and said with hand clapping enthusiasm, "That sounds fantastic." Jamie took their names and phone number.

Jamie, of course, didn't call. Not right away at least. He waited for the group's deadline to pass, and once it passed and the aliens hadn't arrived, Jamie made his move. He called Mr. and Mrs. Lint to see if he could meet with them. Mrs. Lint said they would love to see him. This was the difficult part of Jamie's sales strategy: he had to play the role of a Doomer turned life insurance salesman. It was never easy.

One thing in Jamie's favor was that Doomers, living beyond their own Doomsday, were usually depressed and despondent. They were slightly suicidal and generally grumpy. Some were ready to believe in anything to fill the hole left by their collapsed belief systems.

So, one stormy Monday morning at 9:00 am sharp, Jamie pulled up to the Lint's house. He parked, limped to the front door. He paused for a moment collected himself and repeated the mantra of his profession, "My money is in their pockets. My money is in their pockets," and then rang the doorbell.

Mrs. Lint opened the front door. "Hello," she smiled.

"Hello Mrs. Lint..."

"We've been waiting for you all morning long. Charley is *soooo* excited that you wanted to stop by.."

Jamie noticed that Mrs. Lint was wearing an extra large white t-shirt that read "Goat Foot Pilot." The words were printed in plain black block letters.

Jamie stepped inside and saw that it was a typical Doomer house. It was devoid of all furniture, with the exception of a folding table, a couple of chairs and an old beat up television. No self respecting Doomer would own anything as the end approached. Mr. Lint was seated in a chair at the table. He had a yellow legal pad of paper in front of him. He was asleep.

"Charley, Jamie is here," announced Mrs. Lint. Nothing.

"CHARLEY, JAMIE HAS STOPPED BY TO SEE US," she yelled. Still nothing.

"Maybe I can come back at a better time," Jamie suggested.

Mrs. Lint walked over to Charley. She picked up the legal pad and whacked Mr. Lint on the top of the head.

"What the hell..." Mr. Lint woke up swinging. Jamie realized that Mr. Lint was also wearing a white t-shirt with big black letters. His shirt read, "Endless Crapper".

"Charley, Jamie is here to visit with us."

Mr. Lint looked around the room, trying to gather his bearings. He scowled at Jamie, "Who the hell are you?"

"We met at the rally a couple of weeks ago. You were passing out the cookies."

"He's the one I thought looked like Chad," explained Mrs. Lint.

"What the hell do you want?"

It was an uncomfortable beginning. Jamie wiped his brow and said, "Well, I was waiting for the aliens to come. I was waiting to be a vehicle of doom. I really was. My whole heart was in it. And then when they didn't arrive, I got really down. I mean what happened to them? Maybe they're lost...or delayed...or maybe something terrible happened to them. Then I began to think about life. Maybe we won't die. Maybe we are all going to live. Maybe, just maybe..." Jamie began to notice that Mr. And Mrs. Lint's faces were buried deep beneath a set of frowns. *They can smell the sales pitch,* thought Jamie. He decided to take it slower. "Is everything OK?"

"What the hell are you talking about?" asked Mr. Lint.

"The aliens that didn't arrive..."

"These damned shirts were made by aliens."

Jamie tried to smile. "I'm sorry. They were made by illegal immigrants?"

"No. You dumb son of a bitch. Aliens from outer space."

"Didn't you get your shirt?" Mrs. Lint had that concerned motherly look on her face, but she was really imagining hitting Jamie in the head with a meat cleaver.

"Oh, of course. Of course I got it. I just didn't feel like wearing it," Jamie lied.

"You didn't feel like wearing it?" Mr. Lint was beyond words.

"What's your name?" asked Mrs. Lint.

"Jamie," said Jamie. His mind began to send out warning signals. The scene was beginning to freak him out.

"No, your new name. The one on your shirt, silly." Mrs. Lint now hated Jamie more than her son Chad.

Jamie looked at the shirts. Endless Crapper. Goat

Foot Pilot. "My new name? Mule...Snot...Sucker." Jamie was sweating profusely.

"Yeah, well you should be wearing yours. Because you never know when the world is gonna blow – and these shirts are our salvation," explained Mr. Lint.

"Of course," said Jamie. He was completely confused.

"Dr. Rammer explained at the meeting...weren't you there?" Mr. Lint was convinced that Jamie wasn't flying at full speed. "These shirts were given to us by the aliens so that they can identify us. These shirts are our insurance," said Mr. Lint.

What a load of crap, thought Jamie. Then he added with a smile, "To be honest, I just don't like my new name that much. I mean Goat Foot Pilot is a good name. But Mule Snot Sucker?"

"Well at least you're not Endless Crapper," Mrs. Lint joked, but Mr. Lint didn't find his new name very funny.

"It's just unfortunate that the aliens don't know English that good," Jamie laughed. Neither Mrs. Lint nor Mr. Lint thought the comment funny. "Well, anyways...I don't think the world is gonna end today," said Jamie.

"What the hell do you know?" barked Mr. Lint.

"It doesn't look too good outside if you ask me," said Mrs. Lint peering through the curtains.

Jamie limped to the window. The sky was gangrenous green and filled with black pussy soars. Jamie listened at the window. Everything was silent. There wasn't a single sound. Not a buzz. Birds, squirrels, deer, moles, flies, bees – all of suburban nature that lived in the Lints' neighborhood had enough sense to hide.

"Oh, my God," said Jamie.

"You need to run home and get your shirt," advised Mrs. Lint.

Jamie limped quickly to the front door. But the wind was getting wild, and the screen door started slapping violently against the house.

"Maybe I should wait a bit."

"But your shirt? Don't you want to be saved?" asked Mrs. Lint.

Jamie said nothing. He just looked out the window.

"Of course he doesn't want to be saved! He's a bum. Just like all the other dead beats in his generation," answered Mr. Lint.

The wind was roaring. There was a sudden silver flash and then darkness. The darkness didn't last long, but it was profound. Deep. Not a single spark of light could survive in that darkness. When the light returned everything seemed grey and faded. The light seemed stale and tarnished. Standing among the Lints and Jamie was Death.

Mrs. Lint howled. Jamie jumped, and Mr. Lint blurted, "Are you one of the God damned aliens?"

"No, I'm Death," said Death.

Mr. Lint was perplexed. Mrs. Lint shook with fear. Jamie Dropping couldn't believe his eyes. He had always imagined Death as a black robed skeleton with a sickle. But Death didn't look so fierce or ominous. Instead Death looked like a used car's salesman. He was wearing a short sleeve dress shirt and a tie. He was balding and his hair was combed over from one side of his head to the other. Death was even chewing gum.

"You can't be Death," said Jamie.

"Why not?"

"You look just like..." Jamie didn't know what to say, plus he didn't want to offend Death by telling him that he looked like a used car salesmen.

"I look like an insurance salesman?" Death smiled. "I'm Death, Jamie. I don't peddle life insurance." Touché.

"Yeah, whatever," Jamie mumbled to himself. Mr. and Mrs. Lint weren't paying attention to Jamie's conversation with Death. They were busy whispering about the aliens and being saved.

"What are you two whispering about?" snapped Death.

The old couple stopped whispering and Mr. Lint spoke to Death in Tarzanese, "Me Endless Crapper. She Goat Foot Pilot."

Death was not finding the situation amusing. He was grossly irritated by Jamie's doubting and Mr. Lint's profound lack of intelligence.

"Enough bullshit. I have come for you three. As of this moment you're all dead."

Death was carrying a beat-up, tan briefcase. He dropped it on the folding table and popped it open. Inside the briefcase was a chaos of paper. Death sighed at the sight of it and began to rummage through the papers.

It wasn't that Death was disorganized, there was just too much work. He couldn't keep up with it all. He cursed the Universal Governing and Organizing Department for its lack of support. But he knew things would never change. Death was seriously considering subcontracting some of the collection work to some of the Dead in order just to get some time to himself: to watch *Laverne and Shirley* reruns, sipping a Budweiser. He just wanted a break.

Death finished rummaging and swore, "DAMN IT. I only have the long forms left." He sighed, pulled out a pen and asked Mrs. Lint. "Full name please."

"But you can't take my husband or me...we're saved."

"We have the t-shirts," insisted Mr. Lint.

Death looked at the t-shirts. "Death gives preferential treatment to no one."

"But if we're dead, we'll miss the end of the world?" Mrs. Lint was very disappointed that she couldn't watch million of others burn or drown, however Armageddon would play itself out.

"Those are the breaks."

"Is it because of my leg?" Jamie asked Death.

"What the hell are you talking about?"

"I never saw a doctor about my leg going numb."

"Listen people, you're dead. Forget about the living. Forget about what you regret not having done while alive. It just makes being dead more difficult," said Death returning his attention to the paperwork.

"Well...well, I'm not dead," protested Jamie Dropping. He limped quickly to the door. Flung it open and stepped out into the eerie green daylight. He fought against the wind and made his way to his car. He wrestled with the driver side door. Death stood, watching Jamie from the front door – flanked by Mr. and Mrs. Lint.

Jamie managed to open the car door and shouted out defiantly, "Ha."

"You're going to let him get away?" complained Mrs. Lint.

"The car is dead as well," Death sighed.

Jamie turned the key, pumped the gas, turned the key a few more times. Soon, the engine was flooded and stank of gasoline.

Jamie limped back to the house. He tucked in his shirt tails and said, "My car won't start. I need to call a tow truck."

"The phone is dead." said Death. "Your car is dead. These old people are dead. You are dead, Jamie." Death unwrapped another stick of Juicy Fruit and popped it into his mouth.

As Death filled out the paperwork, he kept checking his watch and sighing, "This is ridiculous." Then he made an appeal for sympathy, "Look at the amount of paperwork I have to file. I've got another 155,456 people to collect still. God I hate this job."

Mr. and Mrs. Lint had turned on the TV and were flipping the channels. They wanted to see what was happening around the world. Maybe this was the end of the world. To their surprise nothing was happening. Sports channels televised golf from India, tennis from Australia, there were even people bowling and playing poker. Mr. Lint continued to flip through the channels. He found a talk show where the hosts were discussing the food they ate for dinner the night before. They told jokes. He landed on a channel that showed a colorful parade marching down a street. Drums and trumpets. Batons tossed into the air. Cheerleaders flipped and did cartwheels. He dropped the control from his hands. Mrs. Lint began to cry. It was depressing for them to think that the world still went on even when you no longer existed. It made the Lints feel cheated. It seemed so unfair. You were dead and people were telling jokes, bowling and having parades?

Even Jamie found the images a bit depressing. Seeing the living made him think about his own life. There was a lot of stuff he didn't want to think about. There were parts that he would have liked to flush down the toilet. Whole decades. But even though he had made a mess of the life he had lived he still wanted to go on. He didn't want it to end. While the Lints wept bitterly to one another and lamented the absence of the aliens that should have saved them, Jamie sidled up to Death. "Is there anyway you can maybe let me live?" he sniveled.

"Impossible. You are already dead," Death didn't look up from his paperwork.

"There isn't anyway I could get a second chance or something?"

Death sat back and sighed. He glowered at the Lints. "Frightening. Absolutely frightening. You know, the living scare the hell out of me," Death put his arms behind his head and Jamie could see the sweat stains in the armpits of his shirt. "I've got an ICU02 form. It's a diversion. It's a helluva lot less paperwork."

"A diversion?"

Death rummaged through his briefcase and pulled out another form. "You can be reborn. How's that? You can be reborn anywhere you want. So, think of some place exotic."

Jamie couldn't believe what he was hearing. He was stunned silent. Never in his life had he been so lucky.

"So where the hell do you want to go?"

"How about..." Jamie thought for a moment and said the first place that came to his mind, "Idaho."

"How about Monkey's Elbow Idaho? It's filled with

retired circus performers. Acrobats, escape artists, lion tamers. I always like it there. A real friendly bunch."

"Sure."

Death started filling in the paperwork. Jamie peered over Death's shoulder and watched him write the words *Monkey's Elbow Idaho.*   At the top of the form was the title

ICU02: Soul Diversion

While Death filled out the paperwork and the Lints whispered hotly at one another, Jamie waited to be reborn.

*****

Mr. and Mrs. Lints' nosy neighbor, Mrs. Joy Mudwart, was watching the eerie weather conditions from her front door. She peeked through the curtains with one eye open and the other closed tight. She was afraid of what she might see. Maybe the dead were parading about looking for living humans to eat, or something equally horrible. And what *did* she see? With that one terrified open eye, she saw three skeletons doing the dance of death in the yard next door. She ducked down. Her heart racing, panting. She looked again. Two skeletons dancing and the third sort of limping around. Mrs. Joy Mudwart shrieked, "LESTER!!!!!"

Her husband, Lester, was hiding in the basement, daydreaming about throwing himself off a cliff. "What?

WHAT? WHAT THE HELL DO YOU WANT NOW?" he shrieked back. "Lester, skeletons are dancing in the Lints' front yard. This time the world really is ending, Lester."

THE LABORS OF JAMIE DROPPING

THE LABOR OF FINDING LABOR
(OR IS YOUR JOB MURDER?):
THE JOB INTERVIEW

DOMESTIC LABOR:
WALKING WALTER

THE LABOR OF GROWING UP:
THE FIRST TIME

THE LABOR OF FAMILY:
BARBECUED

THE LABOR OF OCCUPATION:
OOPS INC.

THE LABOR OF EDUCATION:
BLOODY BOOTS BURIED IN THE SAND

THE LABOR OF NOT HAVING LABOR:
THE UNEMPLOYABLES

THE LABOR OF THE END:
THIS TIME THE WORLD REALLY IS ENDING AGAIN